Nowhere to Hide

I turned my eyes from the mountaintop. Something was moving across the ice to my left. It was a figure running quickly over the rocks. My mule had walked slowly on the slippery slope, but this person ran as if he were sprinting through a flat field. The figure headed right for me. I could see the person was large— much larger than me. My heart began to pound. The figure drew closer.

READ ALL THE BOOKS
IN THE **wishbone classics** SERIES:

WISHBONE classics

Frankenstein

retold by Michael Burgan

Interior illustrations by Ed Parker

Wishbone illustrations by
Kathryn Yingling

HarperPaperbacks

A Division of HarperCollins*Publishers*

HarperPaperbacks *A Division of* HarperCollins*Publishers*
10 East 53rd Street, New York, N.Y. 10022

Copyright ©1996 Big Feats! Entertainment
All rights reserved. No part of this book may be used or reproduced in any manner whatsoever without written permission of the publisher, except in the case of brief quotations embodied in critical articles and reviews. For information address HarperCollins*Publishers*, 10 East 53rd Street, New York, N.Y. 10022.

Cover photographs by Carol Kaelson

A Creative Media Applications Production
Art Direction by Fabia Wargin Design

First printing: September 1996

Printed in the United States of America

HarperPaperbacks and colophon are trademarks of HarperCollins*Publishers*
WISHBONE is a trademark and service mark of Big Feats! Entertainment

❖ 10 9 8 7 6 5 4 3

VICTOR FRANKENSTEIN

Introduction

All set to enter a world of action, adventure, drama, and laughs? Then come along with me, **Wishbone**. You may have seen me on my TV show. Often I am the main character and sometimes I am the sidekick, but I'm always right in the middle of a thrilling story. Now, I'm going to be your guide as we explore one of the world's greatest books — FRANKENSTEIN. Together we'll meet a lot of interesting characters and discover places we've never been! I guarantee lots of surprises too! So find a nice comfy chair, and get ready to read with **Wishbone**.

Table of Contents

Mary Shelley

Let me introduce you to Mary Shelley, the author of FRANKENSTEIN. Mary spent much of her life surrounded by famous writers, and she became pretty famous herself! But Mary also had a lot of sadness in her life, just like her two best-known characters, Victor Frankenstein and his monster.

Mary Wollstonecraft Godwin Shelley was born in London, England, on August 30, 1797. Mary's father, William Godwin, wrote novels and books about politics. Her mother, Mary Wollstonecraft Godwin, was also a writer. She wrote a famous book about women called *A Vindication of the Rights of Women*. Mary Wollstonecraft Godwin thought men and women should be treated equally. Unfortunately, Mary Shelley never knew her mother—Mrs. Godwin died just ten days after Mary was born.

Mary's father was friendly with many writers, and Mary grew up listening to their ideas. In 1808, Mary published her first poem. She was just eleven years old! Mary liked to daydream as a child, and that trait helped her as a writer.

As a teenager, Mary met Percy Bysshe Shelley, a friend of her father's. Shelley was a poet. He and Mary fell in love, and in 1816, Mary and Shelley got married. Mary had five children with Shelley, but only one lived to become an adult. Having lost her own mother at a young age and having to cope with the death of her own children, Mary knew a lot about suffering.

In 1816, Mary and Percy Shelley traveled to Switzerland. While staying at a friend's house, Mary thought of her idea for *Frankenstein*. She finished the book the next year, and it was published in 1818.

When *Frankenstein* first came out, Mary Shelley's name wasn't on the book. Few women authors could get published in those days. Book reviewers had mixed feelings about *Frankenstein*—some liked it a lot, but others didn't care for it at all. Readers, however, enjoyed its horror and strong emotions. A popular play based on the book came out in the 1820s. About a hundred years later, filmmakers began creating movies based on Shelley's story. Some were true to her book, but some of the films put the monster in odd places like the American Wild West, and even outer space!

Frankenstein wasn't the only thing Mary wrote. She also wrote other books, short stories, and articles. In 1822, Mary suffered another great loss when her husband drowned in a boating accident. Mary never remarried, and her writings helped support her and her son. She also edited books of her husband's writings.

Mary Shelley wrote her last book about fifteen years before her death in 1851. Today, none of Shelley's books is as well-known and loved as her first work, *Frankenstein*.

You may have heard about Victor Frankenstein and his monster. Over the years, a lot of movies have been based on Mary Shelley's book about the young scientist who creates a living being. But not many people know the book itself. Mary Shelley was just eighteen years old when she started writing it—practically a pup! And she got the idea for the book on a rainy night in Switzerland—a scene almost as spooky as some in the book.

Mary Shelly, her husband Percy Bysshe Shelley, and some other guests were staying at a friend's house. They spent some of their free time reading ghost stories. One stormy summer night, the host suggested everyone write their own scary story. Mary thought about this for a few days. Then one night while lying in bed, she had what she called a "waking nightmare"—she wasn't asleep, but what she saw was like a dream. What Mary saw gave her the idea to write *Frankenstein,* the story of a young scientist who assembles body parts from dead people and brings them to life.

Mary Shelley wasn't the first author to write about people creating living beings from dead material. The ancient Greeks, who lived thousands of years ago, told stories about creatures made from gold, and one well-known Jewish folk tale describes the *golem,* a monster made from clay. But today, Victor Frankenstein is the most famous creator of a living creature.

Mary originally planned to write a short story, but her husband suggested she write a whole book. Percy Shelley also helped Mary edit, or rewrite, parts of the book. At one time, some people thought he may have written *Frankenstein,* but the experts now agree that Mary wrote the book.

Frankenstein is called a horror story, but some literary experts say it's science fiction too—maybe the first science fiction story ever. It introduced the character of the "mad" (crazy, not angry) scientist who wants to change the world with a daring new experiment. Every mad scientist has an experiment that goes wrong—just like Victor's did. Mary Shelley may have thought she was writing a simple horror story, but her book has influenced a lot of creative people since 1818.

MAIN CHARACTERS

Victor Frankenstein — a young scientist who creates a living creature from dead flesh

The Monster — Frankenstein's creation

Captain Robert Walton — an explorer seeking the North Pole

Elizabeth Lavenza — Victor's adopted sister and later his wife

Henry Clerval — Victor's best friend

Mr. and Mrs. Frankenstein — Victor's parents

Ernest and William Frankenstein — Victor's younger brothers

Professor Waldman — Victor's chemistry teacher

Professor Krempe — another of Victor's science teachers

Justine Moritz — a family servant of the Frankensteins

Grady — Captain Walton's assistant

SETTING

Important Places

The Arctic Ocean — ocean surrounding the North Pole

Geneva, Switzerland — Victor's hometown

Ingolstadt, Germany — site of Victor's university

The Alps — western Europe's longest and highest mountain range

Northern Scotland — site of one of Victor's experiments

Time Period

Frankenstein takes place in the late 18th century (1700s). Life had changed greatly in Europe during the previous fifty years. In England, the invention of the steam engine and other powerful machines led to the first factories. For the first time in history, large numbers of people left their farms to work in cities and growing towns. This "industrial revolution" spread across the world.

The late 18th century was often called the "age of enlightenment." Democratic ideas spread quickly, especially after the American and French Revolutions. Many great thinkers believed humans were basically good, and science could solve all the world's problems. The scientists studied electricity and made great discoveries in chemistry too. Adventurers continued to explore lands that Europeans had never seen before, such as Australia and parts of Africa. In general, most educated people believed in a better future for all.

But some thinkers and artists saw a dark side to science and the Industrial Revolution. These people, called Romantics, thought Europeans needed to remain close to nature. Mary Shelley and her friends were Romantics, and they explored the dangers of the new "enlightened" era in their art.

1
Strangers on the Ice

Our terrifying tale begins in the icy waters just south of the Arctic Ocean. You're about to meet two great adventurers. One wants to find new lands. The other wants to find the secret of life. Robert Walton is an explorer. The mysterious man he'll soon meet is a scientist. Both men are going to learn that sometimes grand experiments or great adventures can go wrong—monstrously wrong. Get ready for the exciting story of FRANKENSTEIN.

Robert Walton watched his crew scurry around the deck of the ship. The men tightened ropes and prepared the sails. Walton pushed his hand through his short blond hair and smiled faintly. His great adventure was finally about to begin.

"Almost ready, Captain," Grady said. Grady was Walton's assistant, a strong man of twenty-five—just a few years younger than the captain. He shared Walton's passion for adventure. Like his captain, Grady hoped this trip would make them famous for their bravery and skill.

"I've dreamed about this day since I was schoolboy," Walton said, staring out over the ocean. "I've always wanted to be an explorer. Now I know we can be the first to reach the North Pole. I want to understand the power there that attracts the needle of the compass. **Walton is talking about the magnetic north pole—the magnetic force that makes the needle of a**

compass always point north. And if we continue on, perhaps we can find a passage through the Arctic to the Pacific Ocean."

Walton grabbed Grady's broad shoulders. "We can do it all, Grady. Do you believe it?"

"Yes, sir. Of course, sir," Grady replied. "I wouldn't be here if I didn't."

Walton smiled. "Good. We can't have any doubt." Walton looked at the sailors running back and forth across the deck. "What do the men say, Grady? Do they think I'm a little...crazy for taking this trip?"

"Oh, no, Captain," Grady said quickly. Then he looked down. "But they do wonder..."

"Yes?" Walton asked.

"They wonder what will happen during our journey. I've heard some of the men expect the worse. Sailing through the Arctic, the ice could crush the ship into splinters in a second."

"I know," Walton said.

"And if the ice doesn't crush us," Grady continued, "it could leave us stranded for months. The men also talk about the dangers of exploring unknown lands. They say you never know what you'll find in that wasteland."

Many explorers did try to find this shortcut from Europe to the Pacific Ocean. They called it the Northeast Passage. Walton is beginning his trip in the late 1700s. The passage wasn't actually found for about another hundred years.

"But you can never find anything if you don't try!" Walton shouted. "I know I can reach the Pole!" The captain took a deep breath and calmed himself. "I know I can," he repeated. "It's worth every risk."

Walton and his crew sailed from Archangel, a port city in Russia. They headed for the Arctic Ocean. Even though it was summer, ice surrounded the ship. By the end of July, Walton could not help remembering Grady's warning about the dangers of the trip.

A thick fog clung to the ship's masts and rolled down the deck. Gazing through the gray cloud, Walton could barely see the white sails all around him. The ship sat motionless in ice, like a wild animal caught in a cold steel trap.

Slowly, as the day wore on, the fog began to disappear. "That's a good sign, isn't it?" Walton asked Grady.

"It does make it easier to see, sir," Grady replied. "But it doesn't help us with the ice."

Walton heard some of the sailors grumbling, afraid they'd be frozen there forever. Suddenly, one of the men on deck pointed into the distance.

"Over there, Captain! Look!" he cried. "Something's moving on the ice!"

Walton took his telescope and directed it over the icy plain. He saw a team of dogs pulling a sled. Even from that distance, Walton could see the driver of the sled wasn't an ordinary man. The figure was huge, dwarfing the sled he rode in. His thick, long black hair clung to his face like a spider's web. His broad shoulders and massive arms seemed immensely strong. Wrapped

in animal furs, the figure looked like a two-legged beast from some remote part of the earth. Walton followed the man and his dogs until they were just a black dot on the ice. Then they disappeared from his view.

"Who was that?" Walton wondered aloud. "Where did he come from? Aren't we hundreds of miles from land?"

"Aye, Captain, so I thought," Grady answered. "Maybe we're not so far after all."

"When the ice breaks," Walton said, "we should head in that direction."

"*If* it breaks," Grady answered ominously.

But just a few hours later, the ice did begin to break apart. The sailors cheered at winning their freedom, but Walton kept the ship there overnight to make sure it was safe to sail.

In the morning, Walton came up on deck and saw

the sailors standing along the rail on the side of the ship. "What's going on?" he demanded.

"Look, sir." A sailor pointed to a chunk of ice drifting toward the ship. Walton saw a team of dogs lying on the ice. All but one were dead. Next to the dogs, a half-frozen man clung to a sled. As the man shivered on the ice, Walton could tell this was not the giant he'd seen the day before. This man's arms and legs were nearly frozen stiff, as if they'd been dipped in plaster. His face was cracked and red from the wind. He struggled to stand, but his weather-beaten, withered body couldn't support his weight. Walton could see the man was close to death.

"Good God!" cried Walton. "Get that man on board!"

2
The Mysterious Guest

First Walton and his men saw a huge figure traveling across the ice. Now, a mysterious, half-dead man appears from nowhere. Who is he, and what is he doing alone in the Arctic?

The sailors dragged the frozen man onto the ship. "He doesn't look good," Grady said to Walton.

"I've never seen a man in such bad shape," Walton agreed.

The man staggered along the deck with a sailor under each arm propping him up. The traveler wore a black fur coat that matched his matted hair. His brown eyes were half-closed from exhaustion.

"Where...where are you going?" the visitor mumbled through frozen lips.

"Toward the North Pole," Walton answered, "and then on to the Pacific."

"Good, good," the man struggled to reply. "Then I'll stay with you. That's the way I'm going too."

Walton's eyes opened wide in surprise. "You mean you'd have gone back to the ice if I'd said we were heading east or south?" Walton turned to Grady. "What a strange man," the captain muttered to his assistant.

Walton now called out to the sailors, "Bring him below deck. Get some blankets and some water."

Walton followed his crew as they dragged the man down the steps. By now, the mysterious traveler had fainted. When the sailors reached an empty cabin, they placed the man near the stove and wrapped him in the blankets.

For the next two days, the man lay on the floor of the cabin. Walton often sat by the man and heard him mumble violently. "Demon!" the man screamed. "Go back, go back! No! Not her. Evil...murderer...a monster!" Walton watched him thrash about wildly.

When the man awoke from his restless sleep, the captain occasionally fed him soup. But most of the time, the man tossed about in his bed, crying about *the beast* or *the monster*.

After a few days, when the guest seemed a little stronger, the sailors moved him into Walton's cabin. Walton studied the man's face. "Look at those eyes," Walton whispered to Grady. "One minute they're calm and bright, but the next minute they are filled with madness. What made him like this?"

"It's the weather, Captain," Grady said. "The ice and the cold can make a man lose his mind."

Walton shook his head. "There's something else. Something terrible has happened to him."

Later that day, Walton sat by the man's bed. The guest slowly opened his eyes after another fitful nap. "Feeling any better?" Walton asked, wiping sweat off the man's forehead.

"A little," the man mumbled.

"I know I shouldn't bother you," Walton said, "but I must know." He leaned closer to the groggy man. "Why are you up here alone, traveling across the ice?"

The man struggled to sit up in his bed. "Searching...searching for someone," he said slowly. Walton could hear sadness in the man's weak voice. "Someone who fled from me."

"This person you're looking for," Walton asked the man, "is he traveling by sled too?"

The man closed his eyes and swallowed hard. "Yes."

"Well, then," Walton said, "I suppose that's the man we saw the day before we met you."

"What?" The guest's face turned pale. "What did you say?"

"The other day," Walton continued, "we saw a man traveling across the ice at a pretty good speed. If you could call him a man. He was a giant, an odd-looking creature."

The man looked at Walton with blazing eyes. "More. Tell me more," he demanded in a harsh voice.

"There's not much to say," Walton said. "The last thing I expected to see was a lone traveler on a dog sled in the middle of nowhere. And then to see you too—"

"Which way?" the man interrupted. "Which way did he go? North?"

"Yes, north, more or less," Walton replied. The man's excitement stirred Walton's curiosity.

"The ice broke the other night," the man continued, now sounding stronger. It was as if the news of the lone traveler had given him new life. "Could the ice have damaged his sled? Could he have survived that?"

"It's hard to tell," Walton said. "He might have found safe ground before then."

The man's face showed disappointment. "I must get up," he said, slowly swinging his legs off the bed. "I want to go on deck. Have to look for that other sled—"

"No, really, sir," Walton said gently, forcing the man back into bed. "You need to rest. I'll have one of my men call if we see anything."

For the next few days, the ship moved slowly past jagged pieces of ice. Walton often stood on deck and peered through the fog, looking for the huge figure on the sled. He couldn't decide if he wanted to see the man or not. Finding the lone traveler might answer some questions, but Walton sensed it could also lead to danger.

When he went below deck, Walton kept a close watch on his guest. The man jumped nervously whenever a crew member entered the cabin. He only relaxed when Walton was there alone. Walton found himself liking the man, despite his odd behavior. The guest was polite, charming, and intelligent. Walton had felt lonely on his voyage. Perhaps, he thought to himself, he'd finally found a friend.

After a few more days' rest, the guest was ready to leave the cabin. He and Walton walked up on deck. The man asked Walton about his trip, and the captain excitedly told him about his explorations. "There's so much I can learn on this trip," Walton said. "I can make history if I reach the Pole. Do you know what that's like, to do something no one else has done before?"

"Yes," the man replied, gazing out into the fog. "Yes, I do. And I wish I had never done it."

Walton was puzzled. "You can't mean that. What about the glory? What about the satisfaction of doing what others say is impossible? I'd give up all my money for that."

He means insane, not angry.

"Stop!" the man exploded. "Are you mad? Don't repeat the mistakes I've made."

Walton stepped back. "What mistakes?" he asked.

The guest ignored Walton's question "I suppose I made you curious the other day," the man said, "when I asked about the person on the sled."

Walton smiled. "Yes, you did. But I didn't want to bother you with questions."

"You think I'm strange, don't you?" the man asked. "You think I'm keeping secrets."

"Well—"

"Here I am, all alone in this frozen desolate wilderness. You find me floating on ice, almost dead. Then I tell you I'm chasing some mysterious figure."

Desolate means lifeless or deserted. A desolate place is usually pretty gloomy. And a person can feel desolate if he or she is all alone and sad.

"A demon, you called him once," Walton said.

The man sighed. His shoulders sagged like he was sinking under the weight of a huge boulder.

"Captain, I have suffered tremendously in my short life. Terrible things have happened to me, and I've done horrible things to others. I once promised I would never tell anyone about the evil I've seen—and done. But you've been so kind to me." The man stopped and looked into Walton's eyes. "I can tell you're like me. You're willing to take risks and do what you think is right. You seek knowledge and truth. But sometimes we seekers can go too far." He paused again. "If you'd like to hear it, Captain, I will tell you my story."

"Yes," Walton said eagerly. "I do want to hear it."

"Is tomorrow all right?" the man asked softly. "I'll tell you everything then."

"Of course," Walton replied.

The man turned to head back to the cabin.

"Sir!" Walton called after him. "We've been together on the ship for days, and I still don't know your name."

The man stopped and slowly turned. "My name," he said heavily, "is Victor Frankenstein."

3
Victor Begins His Tale

Now we have met Frankenstein, the main character of our story. What's he doing in the Arctic? What are the deep, dark secrets he's keeping? What strange tales will he tell Captain Walton?

Victor and Walton met the next day in Walton's cabin. Victor had spent many hours in the cramped room, but he had never noticed the table cluttered with maps and charts or the cases stuffed with books. Victor now saw that most of the books were about explorers and exploration; a few were about science. He remembered the many hours he had spent pouring over thick science books, preparing for his great experiment. Victor had read with excitement, racing to the next page, soaking up the knowledge. Now he shuddered with the thought of his lab and what he had created there.

Outside, icy winds shook the ship's wooden masts. Victor felt the vibrations in the cabin. Walton sat on a small stool near the bed. He tapped his foot nervously, waiting for Victor to begin. Victor sat in a chair by the table. He coughed a few times. Finally, he took a deep breath, brushed his hair from his eyes, and began to speak.

I was born in Geneva, Switzerland. My father served in the local government, and we lived comfortably. I was an only child, and my parents showered me with fine toys and clothes. They always gave me their attention and love.

When I was about five years old, my parents went on a vacation to Italy. When they returned they had a little girl with them. She was about my age and she was the most gorgeous creature I had ever seen. She reminded me of one of the valuable china dolls my mother collected. Even as a small boy, I knew the girl was special. She radiated kindness and warmth. She was, I thought, like an angel.

"Mother, who is she?" I asked shyly.

"Her name is Elizabeth," my mother said, reaching out to touch the girl's hair. Elizabeth smiled slightly and moved toward my mother's hand, like a cat craving its owner's touch.

"Why is she here?" I asked, stepping closer. Her face drew me like a magnet.

"Elizabeth is an orphan," my mother explained. "She has no parents. I found her in a small village."

My father now continued the story. "You see, Victor, your mother talked to the peasant woman who took care of Elizabeth and explained that we could give Elizabeth a good home. The woman was happy to send the girl with us. She knew Elizabeth would have a better life here in Switzerland."

Adopting an orphan was a little easier back then than it is today, especially for wealthy people like the Frankensteins.

The girl stood silently. I just stared at her.

"So," my mother said, "we have adopted her. Elizabeth is your new sister."

Elizabeth seemed as fond of me as I was of her. We soon

became good friends, laughing and playing all the time. As we grew, I felt that Elizabeth and I would always be together. Although we were different in many ways— she liked arts and poetry, while I spent hours exploring nature—these differences didn't weaken our friendship. In fact, I think I actually liked her more because of those differences.

When I was seven, my parents had another child, Ernest, and later a third son, William. My brothers also treated Elizabeth as if she was their real sister, but she always remained closest to me.

As a boy, I also had a best friend named Henry Clerval. Henry loved to pretend he was a brave knight fighting evil dragons or rescuing young princesses. He read constantly about the knights of the past and their brave deeds. Henry always tried to convince me to imagine and play with him, but I didn't have time for it.

"Come on, Henry, leave me alone," I told him once. "I don't want to play with you all the time."

"Why not?" Henry asked.

"It's just that I'm interested in science, and you're not," I said. "You always want to pretend to be some old knight clanging around in armor. *I* want to learn the secrets of heaven and earth."

Henry laughed. "'The secrets of heaven and earth.' Oooh, the great scientist."

"Don't laugh," I said, getting angry. "Someday I *will* be a great scientist." I wanted to keep studying nature: plants, animals, insects, and most of all, the human body. I wanted to know everything about all kinds of life.

I hunted for old books by famous scientists I'd heard about. These men were called alchemists. I devoured every page in their books. Their words stirred my desire to know more about the natural world. **Alchemists were scientists who thought they could find ways to turn lead into gold. They also wanted to create an elixir of life—a potion that could make them live forever. By the 18th century, most real scientists thought alchemists were phonies.**

"What is the secret?" I once asked myself. "How do we live and breathe?" I picked up a rock. "Why is a stone hard and lifeless, while I can think and feel? Someday I will learn what causes illness and death. And someday I'll a find way to help people live forever!"

In my books, I read about strange alchemists who claimed they could create ghosts or devils. *The power to conjure these spirits should not be taken lightly,* one alchemist wrote. *No man knows what horror he may create when he experiments with life and death.* Walton, I tell you as I read those words, a chill started in my spine and crawled throughout my body. The cold that gripped me was as icy as any wind here in the Arctic. But the chill didn't stop me. I tried to imitate the alchemists. I recited their spells, filled with harsh, foreign words I didn't understand. I never pulled a spirit out of thin air, but I clung to the idea of creating life.

When I was fifteen, I saw something that changed forever my ideas about alchemy and science. My family had a summer home near Lake Geneva. One humid night, a terrible thunderstorm rolled in over the mountains. I watched lightning bolts cut across the black sky. Cracks of thunder rattled the windows in our tiny cottage.

"What a terrible storm!" my mother cried.

My brothers clung to Elizabeth, seeking safety. But the storm and its ferocious strength thrilled me. I stepped outside to admire nature's fury. The rain pelted me and I heard branches snapping in the wind, cracking like gunshots.

Suddenly, a flash of light struck an oak tree near the house. I saw the silhouette of the tree against the white bolt of light. The tree looked like a skeleton with fifty arms dancing madly in the wind. Then the lightning was gone. When another bolt crisscrossed the sky, I saw the tree was gone too.

"It's completely destroyed," I whispered to myself. I was awed by the lightning's power.

The next morning, I examined the blackened stump. A friend of my father's, a scientist, was staying at the cottage with us. He explained to me about the power of electricity. In that moment, I realized the alchemists and their theories were foolish. Men didn't need spells and magic to understand the world. Real science was more important. I knew I should go to college and study science. What I didn't know was that one day, my old ideas about seeking to create life would once again fill my head and grab my soul.

Victor fell silent.

"I'm feeling tired, Walton. I must stop now."

"Of course, of course," Walton replied, although he was disappointed. He didn't want Victor's story to end. "Can we continue tomorrow?"

"Yes, tomorrow," Victor said wearily. "If nothing happens before then. Keep an eye out for that sled, Captain."

I don't know about you, but thunderstorms make me head for a nice big bed to crawl under. But for young Victor, a storm gave him an idea: to forget about alchemy and study real science. But what if he used his knowledge to create something... evil?

4
School Days

The next day, Victor is strong enough to continue his story. He and Walton meet again in the cabin, and Victor immediately starts his tale.

When I was seventeen, I prepared to go to college and begin my scientific career. My parents were sending me to the university at Ingolstadt. Before I left, however, tragedy struck and filled me with pain. It was the first time I had ever suffered so much—but it wouldn't be the last.

Elizabeth helped me get ready for my trip. Now grown up, she was even more beautiful than she had been as a child. We talked of how much we would miss each other and promised to write each other every week. As we spoke, I noticed her face was red.

"Are you all right, Elizabeth?" I asked.

Elizabeth wiped her forehead. "It's nothing. I'm just a little warm. Maybe I have a slight fever."

But Elizabeth's "slight fever" was much worse than that. The doctor came and said she had a dangerous disease called scarlet fever. My mother put Elizabeth to bed and I immediately delayed my trip to Germany. Mother began spending all her time taking care of Elizabeth. I often looked in and saw my mother wiping Elizabeth's head or giving her a drink of water. On the third day, I saw Elizabeth sitting up. Her eyes had their familiar sparkle.

"You're better!" I cried, rushing into the room.

Elizabeth smiled. "Yes, I'm feeling stronger," she said. Then she lowered her voice. "But look at Mama. Now *she* doesn't look so well. I'm afraid she's caught my fever."

Elizabeth was right. Unlike Elizabeth, my mother wasn't strong enough to fight the disease. The doctor returned to our house and left shaking his head. "There is nothing I can do," he said sadly.

Her voice trembling, Mother called Elizabeth and me into the room. "I want you two to make me a promise," Mother said weakly. "Elizabeth, I have called you my daughter, and Victor has called you sister, but you know we're not your natural family. Still, I think you two have a special relationship. Do you feel it too?"

I looked into Elizabeth's eyes, as blue as a spring sky. We both smiled and nodded.

"I want you two to marry. Please, before I die, tell me you will marry someday."

I knew these were my mother's dying words, and I fought back tears. But at the same time, Elizabeth warmed my heart. I knew then that what I had felt for her all these years was truly love. "Yes, Mother, of course," I said. "When the time is I right, Elizabeth and I will marry."

My mother's face turned calm as she watched her son and her adopted daughter stand together. Then, she closed her eyes and died. I held in my tears, but Elizabeth's poured down her cheeks.

"It's all right," I told her, putting my arms around. "It's all right. We still have each other. You will always have me, Elizabeth."

After my mother's funeral, I prepared to leave Geneva. I still thought about her often, and I felt empty inside, like someone had stolen the most precious thing in my life. She had loved me so much! But I had to ignore the pain. I had to concentrate on my studies.

Right before I left, Henry Clerval came over to say good-bye. "I wish I were going to Ingolstadt too," Henry said glumly. "We'd have a great time together there."

"I know," I said. "But you can visit me. And write. I want you to keep an eye on Elizabeth and my brothers. Let me know how they're doing. Especially Elizabeth." I sighed. "I'm going to miss everybody."

Henry and I shook hands, then I hugged Elizabeth and my father. I climbed into the carriage and watched the three wave as the horses began to trot down the road. My family and best friend slowly faded from view. I looked around the carriage. It was empty, except for me and my bags. For the first time in my life, I felt completely alone.

After traveling for almost two weeks, I arrived at Ingolstadt. The town bustled with students and merchants, and a tall, white church steeple towered over the main street. My carriage rode past the church and the cemetery nearby. I found myself staring at the gravestones neatly lined up in the yard. *Life and death,* I thought, *I must find the key to life and death.*

The carriage dropped me off at a rooming house, and I took my bags upstairs. My room was small. The bed sat along one wall. Opposite it, a window looked out over the street below. I put my bags on the rickety table in the middle of the room. Two chairs were placed around it. Even at midday, the room seemed dark and gloomy, like a curtain was shading the light. After I unpacked, I left to meet my new teachers.

The first one I saw was Professor Krempe. He taught natural science. The short man slouched over his desk, and his uncombed hair flew out in every direction. When he looked up, I cringed. He was a repulsive little man with a squat nose and beady eyes.

"So, Frankenstein, tell me," Krempe mumbled. "What kind of books did you read to prepare for college?"

"Well, sir," I began slowly, "for a few years, I liked to read the alchemists. But I—"

"Natural science" was a general expression for sciences like biology, which is the study of plant and animal life, or physics, which is the science that explains how things work.

"What?" Krempe shouted. "You wasted your time on those fools? I thought you wanted to be a *real* scientist."

"I do, I do," I assured him.

"Well, then you'd better forget all their crazy notions," Krempe said, snorting with disgust. "Everything the alchemists believed was wrong. Wrong! You're going to have to start all over again with your learning."

I was very upset as I left Krempe's office. I didn't care for his arrogant manner and harsh words. Next I visited Professor Waldman. Waldman was an expert in chemistry. He wasn't much taller than Krempe, but he stood straight and had sharp, darting eyes. I immediately felt more comfortable with him. Waldman spoke kindly, but he also shook his head when I mentioned the alchemists.

"Those men tried to be scientists," Waldman explained, "but they wanted to do the impossible. We modern scientists don't tinker with trying to turn lead into gold. And of course, there's no secret potion that will make people live forever."

"I understand all that now, Professor," I said quickly.

"Scientists study the world as it is," said Waldman. "We don't try to create a world that can never exist, like the alchemists did. But we can still do new and wonderful things. We've learned how blood circulates through the body, and about the gases in the air we breathe. I think our knowledge has no limits. I hope you have a thirst for that knowledge."

I glowed inside as I heard those words. Waldman was speaking about just what I wanted to do—explore new ideas, search for answers. I wanted to do amazing things that no other scientist had done before. I wanted to understand the power of nature and use it to uncover the secret of life. "Can I see your lab, Professor Waldman?" I asked.

He took me into a room filled with mysterious devices. I saw strangely colored liquids bubbling in glass containers. Metal tubes and wires twisted over the glass. Waldman explained what equipment I should buy and what books I should read. By the time I was ready to leave, I knew I had to study with him and learn everything I could about chemistry. He agreed to give me extra teaching in the lab.

"You'll need more than chemistry to be a true scientist," Waldman told me. "Natural science, math— they're all important. But if you work hard, I'm sure you can do wonderful things."

Now I curse the day I saw that lab. Like you,

Walton, I craved glory. But my science only brought pain and destruction.

Victor seems like such a good student, dedicated to learning. What secrets will he uncover? And how could his work lead to pain and destruction? Is all this tied up with the huge, mysterious figure on the sled? Keep reading to find out!

5
The Great Experiment

For the next two years, Victor studied with Professor Waldman. Victor also learned anatomy—the science of how all the body's parts fit together and work. But as he studies the wonders of life, Victor also comes close to death.

My work went well. I was a fast learner, and I won some fame at the school for improving some of the instruments used in the lab. But eventually my class work bored me; I had learned everything the professors could teach me. I turned back to that old question I had always asked myself: *How does life begin?* I realized that to answer that question, I had to do new research on my own. To understand life, I had to explore death.

Late at night, I began sneaking into cemeteries and morgues. **Spooky! Morgues are places where dead bodies are brought before they're buried. Morgues are pretty gloomy places.** Being around the dead didn't bother me. I easily strolled through the graveyards at the blackest hour of night and touched the cold gravestones that dotted the ground. Then I dug up graves and examined the dead. I studied the flesh as it decayed. I looked at every mark on the stiff, blue corpses. I watched worms crawling into

Very spooky! A corpse is a dead body.

rotted skulls and slithering through the remains of brains.

Do you think I'm mad, to talk about these things, Walton? It must seem gruesome to you. But to me, the graveyard was just another classroom. I studied the dead the way you might study a book. Nothing I saw sickened me—I examined bodies that were hacked to death by madmen, and bodies that were destroyed by horrible diseases. All I thought about was the knowledge I gained.

As the weeks went by, I gathered new bits of information about life and the human body. I combined this knowledge with what I had learned in class. Suddenly, I felt like a powerful light erupted in my brain. I had the answer. Other scientists had studied nature and man, but only I knew the secret. **What's the secret, what's the secret? Not so fast. Victor doesn't want Walton to know the details of his theory. Some things are too dangerous to know.** All my hard work led to this one incredible thought. I couldn't believe no one ever realized this before! I could take something dead and bring it back to life. I could create a living being!

I didn't share my knowledge with anyone. I had to test my idea first. If everything went well, then I could tell the world. If something went wrong, it was better if no one else learned about my work.

I started working right away. On foggy nights, I returned to the graveyard, looking for the freshest graves. I shoveled away the moist dirt and took body parts from the corpses. Then I snuck into the dissecting rooms at school, where the medical students cut into bodies. I snatched the organs and veins that would fill my creation. I imagined this being standing in front of me, praising me as its creator.

However, at times I loathed my work. **To loathe is to**

hate something very much. "Am I crazy?" I wondered aloud. "Should I be doing this?" But my desire to test my theory, to do what no one else had done, was like a whip pushing me forward.

The summer was beautiful that year in Ingolstadt. The sun shone brightly almost every day and the fields seemed to glow bright green. But I didn't see nature's beauty. I worked in my lab—a small, abandoned room at the top of my building. At night, I returned to the cemeteries and morgues. I barely ate, and my body wasted away like the corpses I once studied. My skin turned sickly white. I couldn't sleep; my mind raced with thoughts of my creation. A weaker man might have collapsed from exhaustion, but my dream of creating life kept me going.

One night, I was writing in my notebook by candlelight. My eyes began to burn as I fought sleep. The words on the page blurred. I closed my eyes for a second and my head filled with images of arms and legs and organs. I could feel my entire body go numb.

Death, I heard a voice whisper in my brain. *You know death.*

Suddenly, a noise shook me from this trance. "What was that?" I said nervously to myself.

I jumped up from my desk and paced around the little room. Even the smallest sound jolted my nerves. Had someone crept into my room while I nodded off to sleep? I searched under my bed and behind the curtain. Nothing. Then I heard the sound again—a quick, hard rattle. I sighed with relief.

"It's just the wind," I assured myself, going over to the window. "Just the wind against the glass."

All my hard work was making me tired and sick. I ended each day with a fever, and I felt like my mind could snap at any moment. But I had to finish my work.

The few times I did go out during the day, my classmates noticed I had changed. They whispered among themselves when I passed by. "Look at Frankenstein," I heard someone say. "He never leaves his room."

"He looks awful," another student said. "He's so pale. Like he's near death."

"Something odd is going on in that lab where he works," the first student said suspiciously. "Something he doesn't want us to know about."

I didn't care what the other students thought. My creation was almost done. That night, I took my tools to the lab, ready to give my creation a spark of life. Rain pounded on the windowpane. Outside, the wind bent the bare trees. They swayed violently, like gray dancers moving to a wild rhythm.

I shook with fear and excitement as I walked up the stairs. In my lab, I studied the being stretched out before me. Then I set up my tools and began to work. The hours passed quickly and I worked late into the night. My mind was sharp and my hands were nimble, like a master sculptor at work. I could feel my heart pounding, ready to explode from my chest. I wiped sweat from my face. The tiny room was warm, and my nose burned from the smell of chemicals. The candle was almost out. I could barely see by its faint glow.

"Almost done," I said to myself. "My moment of greatness is here. All my study has led to this. If it's going to work, let it happen...now!"

I anxiously stood over the creation, watching for movement. Then I felt something stir by my leg. It was a gentle touch, like a baby's. I stared at the creation's shut eyes and the scars that zigzagged across his face.

"Can it be?" I asked.

A dull, yellow eye slowly opened. Then another. I held my breath as the being's body twitched. I finally exhaled, and the creation took his first breath.

"It's true!" I cried gleefully.

The being took another breath. Then, his body began to jerk wildly on the table, his arms and legs shaking violently.

"I've done it," I said. "It's alive!"

I fumbled with a match so I could light a new candle. The creation rolled his head from side to side on the table. I took the candle and held it up to the huge figure in front of me.

I jumped back in horror, fumbling with the candle. Even in the dim light I knew: The thing breathing in front of me was a hideous creature. When I had chosen my body parts, I tried to select the best arm, the perfect leg. During my long hours of work, I'd never thought about my creation as a whole person. Now, the pieces were assembled and life flowed through my creation's body.

I had made the being large, about eight feet tall. His huge arms and legs drooped off the table. The creation had yellow, shriveled skin, patched together like a quilt made from scraps of different fabrics. The patchwork skin barely covered the muscles and veins underneath it. The beast had dark black hair and shiny, white teeth. But the teeth seemed out of place beneath the two yellow eyes that bulged from their sockets. Surrounding the glistening teeth were dark lips, as black as coal.

My legs wobbled as I examined the revolting thing in front of me. Terror and pain filled my heart.

"What have I done?" I shouted. "Two years of work to create this—this ugly *monster!*"

The creature's yellow eyes blinked slowly. He looked up at me. I stepped back. Disgust filled every inch of my body. Before the creature moved again, I bolted from the lab.

6
Terror in the Room

Most people think "Frankenstein" is the name of the monster Mary Shelley wrote about. But as you now know, Frankenstein is the monster's creator. Actually, the monster doesn't have a name, which is kind of sad.

I ran down the stairs and into my room. All I could see was that hideous face staring up at me. How could I ever create such a thing? My excitement was crushed the instant the monster opened its watery eyes. Now I only felt disappointment and disgust.

I climbed into bed but just stared at the ceiling. Whenever I closed my eyes, all I saw was that yellow, scarred skin, and those lips like two thin, black bugs. I tossed and turned for hours before finally nodding off.

In my dreams that night, I saw Elizabeth. She looked so happy and beautiful, with her blushing cheeks and bright blue eyes. In the dream, I ran to embrace her. But as my lips touched her cheek, I realized the woman wasn't Elizabeth at all. It was my mother! Elizabeth's bright clothes had turned into a black shroud. **A shroud is a blanket that's sometimes used to wrap up dead people before they're buried.** I looked at the shroud and saw something moving in the folds of the cloth. I peered closer.

"Worms!" I cried out in the dream. "Worms from Mother's grave!"

The worms crawled in and out of the fabric. I jumped back in disgust.

Seeing the worms shook me from my sleep. I trembled in fear. "Such a horrible nightmare," I said to myself. I turned to look out the window. The rain had stopped, and the moon shone faintly through the clearing clouds. The light entered my room and cast eerie shadows on the walls. The slats on my chair made a shadow that looked like bars on a cell. I heard the last drops of rain roll off the roof and hit a puddle on the street. Normally, the sound of the water comforted me, but tonight it made me think of blood splattering on stone. I turned my head again, and my heart skipped a beat. I saw a shape at the foot of the bed.

"Who—who is it?" I called weakly. "Is someone there?"

Slowly I looked down at the end of my bed. The creature stepped out of the shadows and towered over me. The monster opened his mouth and tried to speak, but he could only utter harsh sounds. My teeth chattered with fear. The beast peered at me with his yellow eyes, then reached out toward me with long, thick arms. I pulled back under my blankets, my skin crawling. I wanted to shout, but my throat was too tight to utter a sound.

The monster took a step forward. He tried to speak again. This time the voice was louder, more threatening. I didn't wait for the creature to come any closer. I shot out of bed, ducked under the monster's outstretched arm, and bolted out of the room.

I sprinted outside, stumbling as I ran. I looked back once. The beast wasn't in sight. I ducked into a courtyard near my rooming house. I listened for the sound of heavy footsteps. The night was quiet, except for some church bells ringing in the distance.

For the rest of the night, I paced around the courtyard, crazy with fear and disgust. I expected to see the creature's distorted head looming over the wall. Whenever I closed my eyes, I saw the beast again, reaching out with those monstrous arms. I knew I had created something more hideous than any monster that torments people in their nightmares.

"And I created it," I said to myself, shaking my head. "I wanted to do something wonderful, and instead I created that thing." I buried my head in my hands.

The clouds returned during the night, and the morning was gray. Around six o'clock, I left the courtyard and started walking aimlessly around the city. I didn't want to return to my room. My heart still raced, and my head pulsed with thoughts of the monster. I kept my eyes glued to the ground, afraid to look around me.

Wandering in this daze, I ended up in front of one of the city's bigger inns. I watched a carriage clatter up the street. "Victor!" someone called from inside the carriage. I jumped when I heard my name. "Is that really you?" the same voice continued.

The carriage stopped. I watched the passengers get out. Then I saw him. "Henry!" I cried. "Henry Clerval!" My tense body relaxed for the first time in months. Seeing Henry's face made me smile.

"I hope you don't mind that I didn't write first," Henry said. "I wanted to surprise you. Though from what Elizabeth says, it sounds like you're not reading much of your mail. What've you been doing?"

"Nothing, nothing, really," I mumbled. I couldn't begin to tell Henry about my experiment and its ghastly result. I knew even my best friend would call me a madman.

"What a coincidence that you were right here when I got in," Henry said warmly. "I'm glad to see you after my long trip."

"Henry, I'm glad to see you too." I put my arm around my friend's shoulder and tried hard to forget last night's horrors. "Tell me all about Geneva," I begged. "How are my father and Elizabeth?"

"Everyone's fine," Henry replied. "They all miss you. I missed you too. I finally convinced my father to let me come to school here."

Henry studied me as we walked through the town. "You know," he said, "your family really wishes you'd write more."

I looked away from him. "I know, I know. But I've been busy."

"You're studying too hard," Henry said. "You look terrible. Have you been sick?"

"No, not really." I thought about my frayed nerves and sleepless nights. "Just busy. I've spent a lot of time on an...uh...an experiment. But now it's done." Just talking about my work made me tremble.

"Good," Henry said cheerfully. "Then you can spend some time with me."

We walked toward the college. "Will you show me your room?" Henry asked. "I'd like to get out of these clothes."

"Ah, well, you see..." I thought about my creature lurking near the room. I couldn't let Henry see what I'd done. Even worse, what if the beast was waiting inside?

"Are you afraid I'll think it's too messy?" Henry

teased. I forced a weak smile. "Come on, Victor. Take ↗
there."

We arrived at the rooming house without seeing
the creature. I made Henry wait downstairs. "I'll just be
a minute," I assured him. Henry gave me a puzzled look
as I headed inside.

I moved slowly up the stairs. The wood creaked
with each step I took. I paused every few seconds, trying
to hear any strange noises, like the grunts the monster
had made the night before. Even in the daylight, the
stairway had a gloomy, gray atmosphere that added to
my fear.

I reached the top step and inched along the wall to
my door. My fingers, clammy with sweat, lightly
touched the door knob. I held my breath and put an ear
to the door. All I heard was the faint sound of the
people and horses on the street outside. Summoning up
all my courage, I turned the knob and threw open the
door.

I saw my bed with the blankets tossed off it. In the
center of the room were my desk and all my usual
things, but the creature was gone. I breathed a sigh of
relief and clapped my hands together, like I was
celebrating a victory in a game.

"It's all right," I called down to Henry. "You can
come up."

Inside the room, my relief and happiness
continued to bubble over. I practically danced around
the room, clapping and waving my arms. Henry looked
at me and tried to smile, but I could see his concern.

"You seem very glad to see me," he said, sounding
puzzled.

"Yes, that's it. I'm so happy to see you," I said. *And,*
I thought, *I'm so happy not to see something else.* I began

to laugh. Henry laughed too. But as I laughed louder and harder—like a maniac—Henry stopped. He saw the wildness in my eyes.

"Victor, are you sure you're all right?" Henry asked. "Why are you acting like this?"

I couldn't respond. I just kept laughing, throwing my head back hysterically. Then, as I brought my head back down, I saw something by the doorway. I saw him. The beast entered the room.

"He's here," I cried, smothering my laughter. "He's here!" I pointed to the doorway, fear seizing my body.

"Who's here?" Henry asked, turning toward the door.

"Don't let him get me!" I shouted. "Don't let him—"

The creature grabbed me by the neck. The huge hands, like slabs of raw, yellow meat, began to squeeze. Everything went black.

7
A Slow Recovery

Walton stood up and looked at Victor, who had grown pale as he told his story.

"This is tale is too fantastic Frankenstein," Walton said. "But I see you sitting in front of me, as alive as I am. The beast obviously didn't kill you."

"There was no beast."

Walton's eyes shot up in surprise.

"Now don't misunderstand me, Captain," Victor continued. "I did create the monster I've just described to you, and he did come to me during that first night. But the next day, with Henry standing by me, there was no beast. I just imagined he was there. I passed out, thinking the beast was choking me."

"You must have given your friend quite a shock," Walton said.

"I'm afraid so. But I was lucky Henry was there. As you're about to hear, he saved my life." With that, Victor began his story again.

Henry, of course, didn't know what caused my madness, but he could see I was very ill. I sweated constantly, and even when I was awake I never knew who or where I was. But I spent most of my time in a delirious sleep, fueled by the fever that burned my body. My monster filled my dreams. His yellow face leaned over my head, and his eyes stared at me sadly. Often, I called out during my nightmares. "The experiment," I would murmur. "Wrong, all wrong.... Beast!" I cried. "Go back. Leave me alone! Hideous thing!"

Henry later asked me about my ravings. I told him that's all they were—the wild nonsense of a very sick man. I explained that I had worked many long hours without eating or sleeping. But I still couldn't tell Henry what I had done.

For almost two months, I passed in and out of my nightmares. Henry moved into my room and nursed me back to health. The winter passed slowly as Henry cared for me. Finally, as spring approached, I grew stronger. The nightmares ended and I began eating more. I thanked Henry for everything he'd done for me.

"If there's ever anything I can do for you—" I said.

"Actually, there is one thing I'd like to ask you," Henry said.

I felt the blood drain from my face. Did Henry know about the creature? Had he figured it out from my wild fits?

"Don't look so scared," Henry said with a laugh. "It's nothing terrible. I just wondered if you'd like to write your family. They sent you a lot of letters while you were sick. I wrote back a few times, but I think they'd rather hear from you." **Have you noticed people wrote a lot of letters in the 18th century? For people who knew how to read and write, letters were the only way to communicate. Traveling was difficult, so they couldn't easily visit a distant friend, and no one had phones or e-mail.**

I nodded. "You're right. I kept putting off writing to them even before I was sick. I'll do it."

"Good," Henry replied. "Now, since you're so much better, maybe you'd like to read a letter from your sister."

"Elizabeth?" I asked excitedly. "You have a letter

from Elizabeth?" I eagerly took the letter from Henry. I read it slowly, enjoying every delicate swirl in Elizabeth's handwriting. I hadn't seen it in a long time.

"What does she say?" Henry asked.

"She's worried about my sickness. She wants me to write."

"Well, now you can write her and tell her you're fine," Henry said.

I put down the letter and smiled. "I miss her so much."

"I think that's enough excitement for one day," Henry said, getting to his feet. "Come on. Put the letter away and get some rest. You can write to Elizabeth later."

"Yes, nurse," I said sarcastically. I stretched out on my bed. For the first time in months, I fell asleep with a pleasant picture in my head. Instead of the ugly creature bearing down on me, I saw my beautiful Elizabeth.

When I was completely healthy, Henry suggested I get rid of all the scientific equipment in my room. Most of my things were still in the lab, but some test tubes and chemicals cluttered my desk. Henry saw how upset I got whenever I stared at them. Sometimes just thinking about science made me shudder. I took Henry's advice. I didn't want to be reminded of my old experiment and what I had created.

But I couldn't totally avoid my past. When I walked through the university with Henry, I often ran into my old professors. Seeing Waldman made me cringe. When I introduced him to Henry, Waldman tried to pay me a compliment. "Ah, Mr. Clerval, your friend Mr. Frankenstein is quite the scientist."

"Really?" Henry asked, interested to hear more. I uneasily shifted my weight from one foot to the other.

"Yes," the professor said. "He's improved some of

our equipment and excelled through his school work. Now I hear he does experiments on his own."

"It's nothing, really," I mumbled. "Nothing at all."

Waldman's words felt like a needle jabbing my heart. I just wanted to forget my terrible past. I wanted to pretend I'd never spent all those nights in the graveyards and the lab. If only I could erase the memory of the terrible thing I created!

Almost a year passed. Henry and I worked hard in school. I took classes with him, studying foreign languages and history—anything but science. In our free time, we spent hours walking through the countryside near Ingolstadt, or attending dances and fairs in the local villages. I hadn't been this happy since I was a boy playing with Elizabeth back in Geneva.

After one of the town dances, Henry and I went back to my room. We laughed and sang like children as we walked through the streets. When I opened the door to my room, I saw an envelope on the floor. The address was written in my father's handwriting. But something was wrong. Henry saw me frown. "What's the matter?" he asked. "Who is it from?"

I studied the envelope. The letters weren't in my father's usual neat style. The writing looked more like a childish scrawl. A black cloud in my head suddenly blocked out my happiness. "I have a feeling," I said, "that this letter contains bad news."

The monster is just a distant memory, and Victor is finally healthy and happy again. But now, he receives this mysterious letter from home. Does the letter contain bad news? Read on to see!

8
A Tragedy—
and a Discovery

I tore open the envelope and quickly read through my father's words. "Dear God!" I cried. I dropped my arms and my whole body sagged.

"What's the matter?" Henry asked, grabbing my arm.

"M-my brother," I stammered. "He's dead. Little William is dead!" I slumped into a chair. Henry came over and took the letter from my hand.

"Was he sick?" Henry asked. "Was there an accident?"

"I don't know," I said, fighting back tears. "I didn't read that far."

I took the letter back from Henry and struggled to focus on the words. I still remember exactly what my father wrote:

Last Thursday, your brothers, Elizabeth, and I went for a walk in the woods outside Geneva. Your brothers went off on their own to explore. Around sunset, Ernest came back by himself. He told us William had run off while they were playing hide-and-seek, but Ernest couldn't find him. We went to the house, thinking he might have gone there by himself. No William. We returned to the field with torches and searched all night. Finally, about five in the morning, I

51

stumbled over something. When I looked down, I saw poor William's lifeless body at my feet. I nearly fainted from the shock.

The doctor examined him and said William had been strangled. The doctor found black marks on the boy's neck. And it appears the killer stole something—a small necklace Elizabeth had given William just hours before he disappeared. The necklace had a picture of your mother on it.

Elizabeth is devastated by the murder. She wants you to come home immediately. She cries all the time, and she thinks she killed William. Not directly, of course. But she did give him the necklace, and she thinks the murderer killed William to get it. Please come to Geneva as soon as possible.

The news knocked the breath from my lungs. I covered my face with my hands. Henry picked up the letter and read it. When he finished, he tried to comfort me. "What can I say, Victor? This is dreadful news. I'm so sorry." He bowed his head. "What will you do now?"

I went to the closet and pulled out a suitcase. "I've got to go home right away. Will you come with me to get a carriage?"

"Of course."

We walked silently through the city streets. All I could think of was William's limp body. What kind of sick person could murder an innocent young boy? And for a piece of jewelry!

At the carriage stop, Henry waited with me until the horses were ready. I didn't say a word as I shook Henry's hand and the carriage drove off.

I spent most of the ride silently staring out the

window. Even the thought of seeing Elizabeth again couldn't cheer me up. Day and night, as the carriage rumbled closer to Geneva, I sensed something terrible was going to happen. William's death wouldn't be the end of my sorrow. I couldn't prove it, but I felt as if evil was all around me. Now, I realize that I never could have guessed all the horror that would eventually fill my life.

At night, the darkness stirred my fears even more. My dread began to melt the calmness I had felt with Henry during the past year. It was as if a raging fire inside me was destroying all the good in my life. Only the familiar countryside helped ease my worry. As the carriage got closer to the mountains, I knew I was almost home.

Finally, I arrived outside Geneva. The city gates were closed. **Many cities used to have walls surrounding them. The cities closed the gates at night to keep out strangers.** I knew of an inn a few miles away and went there for the night. When I got to the inn, I was still upset and frightened. I lay in bed, but my body twitched, as if electricity were running through my skin. I got up and paced around the tiny room. My nerves wouldn't let me rest.

Finally, I left the inn and took a walk. Once I stepped outside, something pulled me toward the woods where William had been killed. I had to take a small boat across Lake Geneva to reach the woods. As the boat glided across the water, anxiety churned in my stomach. Usually, the damp air of the lake made me feel peaceful. That night, each breath I took seemed to burn my lungs. The blackness of the water and sky were shattered by a lightning bolt sizzling near the top of

Mont Blanc. **Mont Blanc is the tallest mountain in the Alps. "Mont blanc" is French for "white mountain."**

A storm moved in quickly over the mountains. Thick, gray clouds appeared from nowhere, blotting out the stars that lit my way. Rain fell slowly, then pelted me harder and faster. **Have you noticed it rains a lot in FRANKENSTEIN? Mary Shelley was one of a group of writers called Romantics. They wrote about love and other emotions. The Romantics also thought that nature could influence how people felt. In a Romantic book, thunderstorms and rain help create a mood...a creepy, spooky mood. So when it starts to rain in FRANKENSTEIN, watch out!**

The cold drops stung like insect bites on my bare skin. The boat began to rock as a wind whipped across the water. I'd sailed on the lake many times before, but this was the first time rough water scared me. It seemed like everything I knew and loved was turning against me. Clutching the sides of the boat, my knuckles turned white. By the time I reached the other side of the lake, the storm was raging all around me.

A huge crash of thunder erupted over me, and lightning zigzagged to the ground. The trees almost seemed on fire. During a brief flash, I saw something move behind a tree. I couldn't tell if it was an animal or just a shadow. Then, a gigantic bolt of lightning lit the area in front of me. I saw the shape of a man. Who else would be out in such a violent storm?

Another flash of lightning gave me the answer. I saw the figure's huge shoulders, and the odd, distorted features on his face. The rain soaked his black hair. "The monster!" I cried.

Another flash of lightning gave me a better look at the creature's face. I swore the beast's black lips curled into a devious smile.

"Demon!" I called "What are you doing—"

I stopped. A thought flashed across my mind, as quick and powerful as the bolts darting through the sky. The beast had been hiding in these woods. He must have murdered William! Only a monster could have brutally killed my brother. As I realized this, my legs buckled, and a sudden chill gripped my body.

The beast didn't stay in one spot for long. After the next crack of thunder, he ran toward the mountains. I thought about chasing him, but the monster moved quickly over the wet rocks and disappeared.

I stood there, my legs frozen, as the rain drenched me. The thunder slowly rolled into the distance. I recalled that night in the lab, the night I created the monster. I felt the horror of that moment all over again. For two years, my monstrous creation had roamed through Germany and Switzerland. Was my brother's murder the beast's first crime? I doubted it. I had created a thing that loved destruction, that craved human misery. Because of me, my brother lay in his grave. I shuddered when I thought of the other terrible acts the beast must have committed. "I have to tell the police," I said to myself. "We've got to stop him."

But I soon realized how crazy those words were. How could I tell the police I had created a being out of dead body parts and skin? How could I say that I had brought the creature to life, and now it had murdered my brother? I knew how absurd it seemed. And I knew I couldn't tell anyone about the murderer—my monster.

Victor feels miserable. He's sure his monster killed William—and maybe other people as well. But what can he do? Who would believe that Victor brought human body parts to life? And if people did believe it, what would they do to Victor? What will Victor do now?

9
The Wrong Killer

**As Victor tells his story, Walton grows more and more
amazed. Let's see what the explorer thinks of what he's
just heard.**

Walton could see Victor's pain as
he talked about his brother's
death. "I'm sorry, Frankenstein,"
Walton said. "The murder of your
brother is a horrible thing!"

"I was devastated at the time,"
Victor said. "I never thought I could feel
such agony. But once my monster was
loose in the world, my suffering never
stopped. You see, the next death was
almost as terrible."

"The *next* one?" Walton asked.

"Oh, yes. My monster was not done with his evil."

After the beast fled from me, I spent a sleepless
night in the cold rain. About five o'clock, I arrived at
my father's house. I waited in the library until the
family awoke. I looked around the room and saw a
painting of my mother. She looked so young and
beautiful. Then I noticed a smaller painting of William.
I fought back tears, and an image of the hideous
monster crawled into my head.

"Victor!"

Ernest's voice chased away the dark vision of the beast. I turned around to greet my brother. I barely recognized him. He had grown into a young man since I had left for school.

"Hello, Ernest," I said quietly. We embraced. I felt the tears on his cheek.

"How is Papa?" I asked heavily. "And Elizabeth?"

Ernest shook his head. "Not good. Father is almost crazy with sadness. He barely eats or sleeps. And Elizabeth keeps blaming herself for what happened."

I felt sickness wash over me, realizing *I* had caused the pain my family now felt. Poor Elizabeth, blaming herself for William's death—she would never know I was the killer, because I had created that wretched beast.

"You should try to cheer her up," Ernest suggested. "I've never seen her cry so much. Even when she heard the police caught the murderer, she—"

"What?" I interrupted." What did you say?"

"The police caught the murderer," Ernest repeated.

My eyes widened. "Caught the murderer? How could they—no, it can't be. I saw him just last night. He was running through the woods like an animal."

Ernest raised his eyebrows. "What do you mean *he*? No, the person the police arrested is a young woman. She's one of our own servant girls, Justine. Can you believe it?"

"No, no, that's terrible," I said, trying to act concerned. I barely heard Ernest's next words. My monster hadn't been caught! No one would know I was his creator. Then my stomach tightened, and I fought the urge to get sick. An innocent servant girl was being accused of a murder she didn't commit! And it was all my fault. "Do you really think she did it?" I asked.

"I didn't think so at first," Ernest replied. "But the

police have evidence. They're so sure she killed William that they're going to put her on trial today. If she's guilty, they'll hang her."

"Tell me what you know about Justine and the murder," I insisted.

"The morning after we found William's body, Justine took the day off from work. She said she was sick. She stayed in bed for days. On the third day, another servant happened to go through Justine's clothes. She found the necklace."

"The one with Mother's picture?" I asked.

"That's right—the one Elizabeth had given William. The girl who found the necklace didn't tell any of us. She took it right to the police."

"And the police arrested Justine," I said.

"Yes. That was all the evidence they needed. When they questioned her, she acted very strangely, like she was hiding something, or felt guilty. The police are sure Justine is the murderer."

Victor shook his head. "I still don't believe it. Papa treats all the servants so well. Why would one kill William? No, I think Justine is innocent." Of course, I couldn't say why I knew Justine was innocent—because I was sure my monster had killed our brother.

Just then, my father entered the room. "Papa!" I rushed over to hug him, then stepped back to examine his face. He looked so old and exhausted. His eyes were red from crying, and he was thin, as if sadness was wasting him away.

"Victor," he said sadly. "It's been so long. I'm sorry you have to come home to—to all this...."

"It's all right, Papa. How are you?"

"Papa," Ernest interrupted, "Victor says he knows who murdered William."

"I know," Mr. Frankenstein said sadly. "That servant girl. I can't understand it."

"No, Papa. Victor says Justine didn't kill William."

My father turned toward me in surprise. "Is that true?"

I fumbled for words. "Well, I didn't say I know *exactly* who killed William. But I can't believe this young girl did."

"So you don't know who William's killer is?" my father asked, disappointed.

I looked down at the ground, afraid to meet my father's eyes. "No, I don't." My face burned as the lie passed my lips. But how could I tell the truth? No one would believe my story about an eight-foot monster. If I explained the experiment and the thing I had created, my father would think I was crazy. *Everyone* would think I was crazy. I had to keep silent.

Elizabeth came into the room. For a brief second, I forgot about the horrible murder and the monstrous creature. Elizabeth's golden hair fell over her shoulders. Even in her sadness, her eyes had a glow of life that made me want to hold her. It had been almost six years since we'd seen each other. She was ten times more beautiful than on the day I had left. We hugged each other tightly. "I feel so much better now that you're home," she said. "Maybe there's something you can do to help Justine. I can't believe she killed William."

"Neither can I," I said, stroking her hair.

"I hate to see a young girl treated like this," Elizabeth went on.

"An innocent person can't be hung for murder," I insisted. "And I'm sure she's innocent. The truth will come out."

"I'm glad to hear you say that," Elizabeth said. She

looked sadly at Ernest and our father. "Everyone else thinks she is guilty. I'd hate to see another person killed for no reason."

Then she began to cry. I wanted to prevent that second death. I couldn't stand to live if another person perished because of my beastly work.

Justine's trial began at noon. Sitting in the courtroom, I squirmed in my seat, filled with agony. Red-hot metal searing my back would have been more pleasant than the torture I felt inside. I wanted to jump up and shout, "Arrest me! Put me in chains! I am the murderer!" Anything would have been better than watching an innocent person hang. But I knew the people there would think I was insane. Everyone knew I was in Ingolstadt when William was killed.

Suddenly, I couldn't bear to stay in the courtroom for another minute. I ran outside.

Later that afternoon, a man I knew came out of the courtroom. "What happened?" I asked nervously. I gripped my hands together so tightly they started to hurt.

"Guilty!" he cried. "The girl confessed. We all knew she did it."

My heart sank to my stomach. Even my own brother's death hadn't ripped at my insides the way this news did. An innocent girl would hang because of me. I rushed home, my head spinning, and told Elizabeth the news.

A few hours later, we received a note from Justine. She wanted to see Elizabeth.

"I'll go," Elizabeth said, "even though she betrayed us."

I went with Elizabeth to the jail. I didn't want to see the girl before her execution, but Elizabeth begged me to go. We walked into Justine's cell and saw her sitting on a straw bed. "I wanted to tell you before they kill me," Justine said as she rose. "I lied. Yes, I confessed, but I didn't kill your brother."

"Why?" Elizabeth demanded. "Why would you confess to something you didn't do?"

"Everyone here in the jail told me it was better to confess. The evidence was so strong against me, and I was confused. They made me think I'm a monster." I jumped when I heard that word, but I kept silent. "I just wanted to tell you again," Justine said, "that I'm innocent. You thought so once, Miss Elizabeth. I hope you believe me now."

Justine and Elizabeth began to cry. I crept into a corner of the cell and watched them weep in each other's arms. I clenched my teeth and moaned. How could I let this girl die? But how could I tell anyone about my monster? The judge would think I was just making up stories about a huge, murderous beast so Justine could go free.

"Sir," Justine said to me between her sobs. "Mr. Frankenstein, do you think I'm guilty?"

Guilt and sadness strangled my voice. Elizabeth answered for me. "No, Justine, he knows you didn't do it."

I nodded. *That's right,* I thought, *you're not the murderer. It was the beast. And it was me, as well.*

The next day, Justine was hanged. I held Elizabeth as she cried. I realized I had caused her suffering too. I didn't imagine then all the pain I would cause her in the future. No, at that moment, all I thought about was that night in the lab. I had wanted to create life. Now, because of me, two people were dead. Who, I wondered, would be next?

When people break a law, they're guilty of a crime. But sometimes you can feel guilty even if you aren't a criminal. Victor didn't really kill Justine, but he feels like he did. If he'd never created the monster, Justine and William would still be alive. Victor's guilt torments him. Can anything make him feel better and ease his troubled conscience?

Helllooo! Start flipping the book pages and check out the action . . . . Woo-cha!

10
The Figure in the Mountains

Many Romantic writers of the 19th century created characters who thought they were going crazy, or had terrible secrets. These writers wanted to explore all the human emotions. Now Victor is going through some very powerful emotions of his own.

The feelings of guilt pressed down on me, it was harder for me to eat and sleep. I felt sickness creeping over me, as it had in Ingolstadt. I spent hours alone in my room. I closed all the drapes and never lit a candle. I wanted to surround myself with darkness, since I felt so black and empty inside. I thought of my dead victims in their graves, and I wanted to feel death myself.

Naturally, my father saw my behavior and it worried him. "Victor, I know you're upset about William," he said to me. "We all still can't believe it. But you can't go on like this."

I didn't respond. I couldn't tell him the real reason for my agony, and my fear that my monster was still terrorizing innocent people. Instead, I kept to myself even more.

Summer came, and my family went to our cottage by the lake. My father hoped the trip would ease our grief. I often wandered alone into the woods, and there I did feel a little better. I tried to spend most of my time outside. At night, I'd sail alone on the lake. But even there, in that peaceful setting, terrible thoughts of the monster still gripped me.

One night, I took the boat and let the wind blow it any direction. The breeze was warm on my face. I heard the frogs croak and the bats flutter their wings as they flew near the treetops. I closed my eyes and tried to think of Elizabeth and how happy we would be someday. But images of the monster pushed her smiling face from my mind. Then I saw Justine, crying in her cell. Tears ran from my closed eyes.

Where was he? I wondered. Where was the beast at that moment? Was he still hiding in the rocks near Geneva? Had he crushed the tender throat of another young child? I couldn't get the monster out of my mind—not that night, not ever. He was always lurking behind every thought, just as he had hidden in the darkness that rainy night by the lake. I realized that the creature was not just a lumbering animal—he was cunning. **That means the beast is smart or clever in a sneaky or nasty way.** Alone on the water, my sadness and guilt boiled together inside me and turned to rage. I had to see the beast again and stop him somehow. I wanted revenge for all the suffering the monster had caused.

I decided I needed time alone, so I took a trip into the Alps. I headed for Chamonix. **Chamonix is a town in the French Alps.** I took a horse, then traded it for a mule as I got closer to the mountains.

I rode along narrow trails in the snow-capped Alps. I listened to the rushing cascades of mountain waterfalls. Once, I heard an avalanche high above me. The snow rumbled and roared like a giant disturbed in his sleep. Up ahead, I saw Mont Blanc. Its craggy rocks cut through the snow like gray trees shooting up through frozen earth. The beauty and power of the icy scene boosted my spirits—for a while. Other times, I got off my mule and threw myself to the ground, filled with despair once again.

After one long day's ride, I found an inn near Chamonix and spent the night. For once, I fell asleep quickly, and my dreams were peaceful.

When I awoke the next morning, I heard rain pounding outside the inn. I looked out the window and could barely see the great mountains. Fog shrouded their jagged peaks. But I didn't care about the weather. I wanted to ride farther into the mountains.

My mule stepped carefully along the paths. Today, nature's beauty didn't calm me. I saw trees almost cut in half by avalanches, and the rocks seemed as sharp as wolves' teeth. The rain and mist painted the sky dark gray. I shivered as I clung to the mule. Finally, I reached a mountaintop below the tallest peaks. Above the clouds, the sun reflected off the top of Mont Blanc. For the first time, some of the day's gloom melted away.

"It's so beautiful here," I said to myself. "So beautiful."

I turned my eyes from the mountaintop. Something was moving across the ice to my left. It was a figure running quickly over the rocks. My mule had walked slowly on the slippery slope, but this person ran as if he were sprinting through a flat field. The figure headed right for me. I could see the person was large— much larger than me. My heart began to pound. The figure drew closer.

"Who is it?" I asked myself. "Can it be—?"

A strange feeling came over me. I thought I might

faint. The figure kept running toward me at full speed. I tried to crouch down behind a rock, but he knew where I was. And he knew *who* I was, just as surely as I knew this determined runner was my wicked creation!

Victor is all alone in the mountains. There's no one he can call for help and nowhere to hide. What can he do?

11
The Creature Speaks

In an instant, the monster was upon me. I froze and held my breath. The beast stopped a few feet in front of me and looked down with his yellow eyes. To my surprise, even with that ugly, evil face so close to me, I wasn't afraid. As I studied the scarred skin I knew too well, all I felt was rage.

"You vile creature!" I shouted, my hands clenched into fists. "You're a devil—a monster. How can you come near me or any human? I wish I could kill you the way you killed my brother. And that servant girl— you're responsible for her death too."

The monster stood there, listening to my angry words. Then, to my amazement, the creature opened his mouth and spoke. "I expected you to be like this," he said in a deep voice. "Everyone hates ugly, terrible things, and look at how ugly you made me. No one wants to come near me. If they do, it's to try to hurt me or kill me."

"I wish someone had killed you!" I spat out the words. "I wish I had done it when you were still on that table in my lab."

"But now it's too late," the monster said slowly and calmly. "Here I am, in front of you again. And I have some things I want to say."

"Why should I listen—"

"Hear what I have to say!" the beast roared. "I want you to do something for me. If you do it, I won't bother you or anyone else again. If you don't, I will kill *all* your friends and loved ones."

"You disgusting, evil thing!" I shouted. Angry beyond all reason, I dove at the monster. The creature easily stepped aside.

"Stop!" the beast cried. "I don't want to hurt you. Just listen to me. That's all I want for now." The monster paused and looked into my eyes. "You are my creator, Frankenstein. I wasn't evil the night I walked out of your lab. But you and other humans have turned me into an evil thing. I've suffered so much. Please, just do what I ask. It's my last chance to be good again."

"No," I said. "I won't do anything for you. I may have created you, but you're my enemy now. Get out of my sight!"

"Please, Frankenstein," the monster pleaded. "Believe me, the being you created that night was good. But you left me alone, you abandoned me. No living creature wants to be alone—even one as repulsive as me. I'm not blind. I know what I look like. If you hate me—you, the man who spent so many nights working to bring me to life—why should any other human feel sorry for me? Now I despise the people who hate me. I detest all humans because of what you've done to me. But you can help me, and make things better."

"No," I said, shaking my head. "I could only make things better if I destroyed you."

"All I want now is for you to listen," the monster said. "Listen to what happened to me after you ran away the night you created me."

"Don't talk about that night," I insisted, throwing up my hands. "I'm sorry I ever started that experiment. I curse the day I stirred life in you."

"Listen to my tale," the monster begged again.

"There's a hut in the mountains. You'll be warmer there. The cold doesn't bother me the way it affects humans. Listen to what I have to say. Then you can decide whether I leave you alone forever."

"Or else?" I challenged the beast.

"Or else I destroy everyone you love."

The monster turned and started walking toward the mountain. I hesitated. Why should I spend another minute with the beast? But I had to admit, I was curious to know what the creature had done during the past two years. And despite the monster's evil nature, perhaps I owed the beast a little compassion. Maybe a creator does have a duty to his creation. I could give the beast a few hours of my time. And maybe I would learn for sure if the monster had killed William.

I followed after the beast. As we reached the hut, a cold rain began to fall. The monster started a fire inside the hut, and I huddled next to it. "You've decided to listen?" the monster asked.

"I have," I said. "Tell me your story."

In the tiny ship's cabin, Walton took a huge gulp of water.

"Your monster can speak!" the explorer said in surprise. "What an amazing creature he turned out to be."

"You will be even more amazed when I tell you everything he said, in exactly his words," Frankenstein promised.

Walton's right—the monster sounds like a bright guy. Not bad for a creature that never even went to school. How did he learn to speak so well? Let's find out what the monster's been up to during the past two years.

12
The Education of a Monster

You know that Victor is telling the story about his monster to Captain Walton. Now the monster is going to tell a story—the story of his life. So, you're about to read a story inside a story. Don't let it confuse you. Just remember, the "I" in this chapter is the monster, talking about what he's done since Victor created him. And the "you" is Victor, who's learning all about his creation for the first time—just like we are.

When you left me that night, I was overloaded with new sensations. Sights, sounds, and smells flooded my brain. I was like a baby exploring a new world. When I closed my eyes, everything went dark, and I was frightened. But when I opened my eyes, I was surrounded by light. So many simple things you never think about I had to discover on my own.

I looked up in the sky and saw a glowing circle— the moon, I later learned. Its light helped me see in the dark night. The wind carried different odors; some were sweet and made my lips turn upward. Yes, even in those first moments, I could smile. But other smells stirred a sick feeling in my stomach and made me want to run. I heard sounds too. To my sensitive ears, the city was like an orchestra with a hundred musicians all playing different songs. All my senses were overwhelmed.

I left the city and spent the night in the forests near Ingolstadt. I shook with cold and fear. I had a coat I had taken from your room, but it didn't keep me warm. I didn't know where to go, and I was so alone. When I felt a stirring in my stomach, I put some tiny red balls in my mouth and tasted a sweet juice. Later I learned they were berries. Everything I did was an experiment. Slowly I learned what I needed to do to survive.

One day, I found the last glowing embers of a fire. I saw that the wood could keep me warm—or burn me if I moved too close. I gathered wood and kept the fire going day and night.

I spent my days looking for wood and food. One morning, I found a small village near the woods. I walked into the first hut I saw. Some children were inside playing. When they saw me, their eyes filled with horror. Their screams brought the whole village running to see what was wrong. Men ran into the hut and attacked me with rocks and sticks. I covered my face with my hands and fled into the woods. What had I done to deserve that? Nothing—except exist. Your experiment created me, Frankenstein, and caused me this pain.

As I ran through the woods, I discovered another small hut next to a much larger cottage. I avoided the cottage and went into the hut. It had a dirt floor, and the ceiling was too low for me to stand, but the tiny room was dry. It was better than sleeping outside, as I had been doing. I decided to stay.

In the morning, I looked outside through a hole in

the wall of my hut and saw a person passing by. It was a young girl with a sweet, smiling face. She wore a simple blue dress and she carried a pail of milk. Then I saw a boy coming to meet her. He was older and taller than the girl. He took the pail and they returned to the cottage. My hut was actually attached to the cottage, and a window in the cottage used to look into the hut. Now, however, the window was covered with wood. But I noticed a crack in the wood. I put my eye up to the hole and could see into the cottage.

The room inside the cottage was almost bare, except for a stool and a fireplace. An old man was sitting on the stool. He had long, silver hair and he held a piece of wood in his hands. The wood had strings on it, and when the man struck the strings, they made beautiful sounds. The young girl ran into the room, and she began to cry as the man played. I heard the sweet melodies and saw the girl cry, and I felt a strange mixture of pleasure and pain. I pulled away from the window. I couldn't stand the emotions flooding over me.

During the next few months, I watched my neighbors as often as I could. I saw them eat, and at night they sat by candlelight and talked for hours. The old man and the children seemed so gentle, so kind to each other. The two children did everything for the old man, who I soon realized was blind. But that didn't stop him from enjoying life, and the three often laughed together as they talked. So many times when I looked at them, I wanted to rush over and share their warmth and happiness. But I knew I couldn't.

I soon learned my neighbors were poor. They didn't have enough food to eat. The two children would give what little food they had to the old man. During my first few days in the hut, I occasionally snuck over to their cottage to steal some of their food. When I saw how hungry the boy and girl were, I stopped. Instead, I just ate the nuts and berries I found in the woods.

I tried to help the family whenever I could. The boy spent most of his time gathering firewood. At night, I would go into the forest and gather wood, then leave it outside the cottage door. You should have seen their surprise in the morning! For me, breaking logs was like snapping twigs, and I gathered more in one night than the boy could in a week. Later, when the ground was covered with snow, I cleared paths for them. I felt very happy helping my new friends.

The most amazing thing I learned was that these people could express ideas with sounds. I learned to speak from listening. The more I listened to them, the more words I could understand. Hearing their words and watching their faces, I could tell when they were sad or frightened. I dreamed about the day I could talk to them and comfort them.

But I knew I had one problem—a problem *you* caused, Frankenstein. When I looked at my neighbors, I saw three beautiful people. They had fair skin and clear, blue eyes. Then, one day, I looked in a pool of water and saw my reflection. I stepped back in horror. I finally understood why everyone shrieked and panicked when they saw me. I realized why even you had left me. Look at this evil, ugly face! How could I ever make friends with the old man and the children looking like this? I was afraid I'd be alone forever.

Some days, the girl, who was called Agatha, seemed very sad. Her brother, Felix, would try to comfort her. I wanted to do the same thing. I wanted to extend my enormous hands and stroke her soft cheeks. But all I could do was watch from my hut. Suddenly, I had an idea. If I could learn to speak well enough to talk to them, they would see I was a gentle creature who cared about them and wanted to be their friend. Maybe I could convince them I wasn't a monster, despite my hideous face. Maybe I could win their love.

I listened even more carefully when Felix began teaching his sister how to read. I saw the shapes printed on the pages of the books and learned how to read too. The books Felix used taught me more about humans and their world. All this knowledge made me realize how odd and foreign I am. I understood that I was a monster, and I cried in agony.

One piece of knowledge jolted me. Felix explained to his sister about mothers and fathers and their children. He said parents love and take care of their babies. I realized I had no parents, no family to love and take care of me.

One day, I made a lucky discovery. Felix left some books outside the cottage. I took them into my hut and struggled to read them. I read history and learned about brave and wise men who ruled distant countries. I also read about love and kindness. Now I had words to describe how I felt about my neighbors. My learning gave me hope, and my heart grew lighter with each passing day.

Soon after this, I made another discovery. I put my hand inside the pocket of the coat I took from your room. I don't know why I'd never looked in there before. My fingers touched a small notebook—your journal. You described every detail of your experiment up to the night when you brought me to life. I finally knew who my "father" was. I cursed you Frankenstein, cursed you for giving me life and making me so ugly!

You had created me, then abandoned me, leaving me completely alone.

I decided it was time to try to make friends with my neighbors. I hoped my education and gentle manner would show them I wasn't a monster. I planned my visit carefully. I wanted to enter the cottage when the blind man was there alone. He wouldn't see my distorted face and sickening skin. If I talked with him and won his affection, then perhaps his children would accept me too.

I waited for a day when the children went out. Then I went to the door of the cottage. I stood outside for a moment, searching for courage. Finally, I knocked.

So far, Victor's monster isn't much of a monster at all. He likes music, teaches himself to speak well, and does good deeds. Unfortunately, people have a hard time ignoring his face. What's going to happen when he enters that cottage?

13
Pain and Revenge

I heard the old man walking around inside. "Who is it?" he called. "Please, come in."

I slowly entered the cottage. "Pardon me for bothering you," I said. "I've been traveling through the woods, and I could use a rest."

"Come in, come in," the man said happily. "I'm glad to have your company. My children are out, and I'm afraid I can't do too much for you. I'm blind, you see."

I didn't say what I thought—that I was counting on his blindness to help me win his friendship. "Don't worry about getting anything for me," I said. "I just want to sit for a while. I don't have any friends, and everywhere I go, people detest me. It's nice to spend time with someone who will talk to me."

"No friends?" the man asked sadly. "I'm sorry to hear that. You sound like a nice young man to me."

"I am, I think," I said. "But people don't look inside to try to understand who I am. They just see my face and think I'm a monster."

"You must have at least one friend," the man said. "Someone you can trust."

I hesitated before speaking. "In a way, yes, I do. I know three good people. I love them very much. I try to help them whenever I can. But they may think I want to hurt them. I hope I can convince them I really am their friend."

"Oh, I'm sure you can," the man said. "Tell me, do these people live around here?"

"Well—" I stopped suddenly as I heard a sound outside. The children were returning.

"Good friend," I said desperately, grabbing his hand. "You and your family are the people I love. Please, tell your children I'm good. Tell them I don't want to hurt any of you. Only you can help me!"

"What is the matter?" he cried. "Who are you? What do you want?"

Felix and Agatha walked through the door. Agatha stared into my eyes then dropped to the floor in a faint.

"What are you doing?" Felix shouted. He pulled his father away from me and swung a stick he clutched in his hand. The stick felt like a butterfly flitting by my head. I could have crushed the boy like an ant. But I wasn't angry. All I felt was deep, bitter sadness. I ran out of the cottage and into the woods.

Alone in the forest, I cursed you again. Why did you make me? Why should I have to suffer so much? You've never felt pain ripping your heart like I did at that moment. I stormed through the woods, filled with hate and longing for revenge. That night, I howled at the stars like a savage beast. I thought just one thing: I hate all humans. A human created me, and humans always made me suffer. I declared war against humans, and one in particular: you, Frankenstein.

The next morning, I crept back to my hut. I expected to hear the family talking inside the cottage. But that morning, the little house was silent. A few hours later, I heard Felix and a strange man talking outside.

"We can't stay," Felix said harshly. "I refuse to leave my father here."

"But you owe three months' rent," the man said. "You still have to pay it."

"I know," Felix said. "You'll get your money. It's worth any price to get away from here."

The family was leaving me for good. Tears filled my eyes. The people I loved had rejected me—just as you rejected me that rainy night in Ingolstadt. My sadness quickly passed, and anger took its place, making my head throb. I remembered my plan to destroy humans whenever I could. Then I thought about my creator, and I focused all my hatred on you. I knew who you were— your name was in the journal I found. And I knew where you were from—you mentioned Geneva and your family there. I wanted to find you.

That night, I went into the cottage and started a fire. I watched the flames creep up the walls, then burst through the ceiling. My anger was as hot and destructive as those flames. As the fire brightened the night, I thought of only one thing: finding you, Victor Frankenstein.

So the monster was rejected by humans once again. If I were Victor, I'd be a little nervous right now. What else does the monster have to tell his maker? Keep reading to find out!

14

The Monster's Request

The monster is telling Victor what turned him into a horrible beast. Here's the last part of the monster's story. He's about to describe what happened as he searched for his creator.

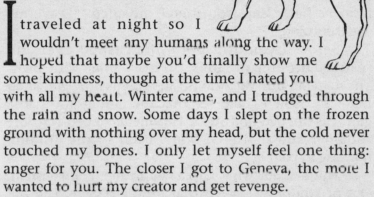

I traveled at night so I wouldn't meet any humans along the way. I hoped that maybe you'd finally show me some kindness, though at the time I hated you with all my heart. Winter came, and I trudged through the rain and snow. Some days I slept on the frozen ground with nothing over my head, but the cold never touched my bones. I only let myself feel one thing: anger for you. The closer I got to Geneva, the more I wanted to hurt my creator and get revenge.

I traveled all winter. When spring came, I dared to walk during the day through some thick woods. It was one of the first warm days of the year, and new life blossomed all around. Birds sang in the trees, which had their first green buds. Crocuses pushed up through the earth, dotting the ground with bursts of yellow and white. **Crocuses are colorful flowers that appear early in the spring.** The warmth and beauty around me actually eased some of my anger. For a few moments, I was happy, and I cried tears of joy. Yes, I still had a trace of joy somewhere inside of me. You humans hadn't drained it all out—not yet.

As I walked through the woods, I heard someone walking behind me. I hid behind a tree and waited for this stranger to walk by. I saw a young girl skipping through the forest. She laughed to herself as she played. In her happiness, the girl didn't see a stream that cut through the trees. She tripped and fell headfirst into the rushing water. I moved without thinking, running to the stream and plucking the girl out. I tried to force water from her lungs and keep her alive.

As I held the girl in my arms, a man came running through the forest. He wore simple clothes and a farmer's hat. "Hey! You there!" he cried. "Leave my daughter alone."

Before I could respond, he rushed over and snatched her from my arms. His face burned with anger. The man ran into the woods carrying his little girl, and I followed. Now I could see that the farmer also had a gun. He stopped and fired. Hot metal ripped into my shoulder and shattered bone. I fell to the ground, howling in pain.

Think about what happened to me, Frankenstein. Out of kindness, I saved that little girl's life. Did her father express any happiness or show me any kindness in return? No. He shot me, tried to kill me, as if I were a wild beast. I realized no human would ever thank me for my compassion or reward me for a good deed. I would always be a monster, no matter what I did. I cursed the injustice of my life. My hatred and desire for revenge returned even stronger than before.

My wound took a few weeks to heal. In the meantime, I kept going toward Geneva. One evening near sunset, I entered a field outside the city. I saw a beautiful young boy running across the field. Seeing him, I had an idea. Even though I was angry at all humans, I still hoped I could find one friend. I needed to find someone young and innocent. Maybe a child wouldn't think I was evil just because I was ugly. A young boy like this one might see the goodness inside my monstrous body. I decided to take the boy and make him my friend.

I ran ahead in the field. When the boy came by me, I grabbed him with both hands and lifted him toward my face. "Don't shout," I said to him gently. "I don't want to hurt you. Please, listen to me."

The boy squirmed violently in my hands. "Let me go!" he shouted. "You monster! Beast! I've heard about ogres like you. You want to rip my body up and eat the pieces. Let me go!"

"I'm not an ogre," I said. "I just want you to come with me."

"No! I'll yell for my papa," the boy threatened. "He's an important man in Geneva. He won't let you eat me."

"You will never see your father again," I said harshly. "You must come with me."

"You can't keep me My father will have you arrested. Everyone knows Alphonse Frankenstein."

"Frankenstein!" I cried. I felt like the boy had stabbed me in the eye. "You belong to my enemy. You shall be my first victim!"

The boy kept shouting and struggling to break free. My hands slid from his shoulders to his throat. Anger boiling inside me, I squeezed. His shouts stopped. In a few seconds, his tiny feet stopped kicking and his body went limp in my hands. I dropped him to the ground.

I stood over my victim. I felt like I had just won a great battle. I clapped my hands. "Look at my power," I said joyfully. "I can create too—create destruction. This is just the first act of my revenge."

I looked down at the dead child and noticed something around his neck. I bent down and saw a tiny painting of a woman. I grabbed the necklace and examined the picture. The woman had dark eyes and long eyelashes. I admired her beauty. Then I remembered I would never have such human beauty in my life, and my anger returned.

I left the boy there and searched for a place to spend the night. I found a barn and crept inside. I was surprised to see a young girl sleeping on some straw. She was another innocent person, like the boy. But she was a human, so she could never be innocent in my eyes. Wouldn't every human who saw me scream at me, call me names, and try to hurt me? I decided I would make this girl suffer too.

I didn't have to attack the girl to hurt her. You see, when I read those books back in the woods, I learned about the small ways a being can do evil things. All I had to do was make it look like she had murdered the boy and stolen the necklace. Her life would be ruined. Perhaps she would even die for the crime I committed. **That innocent girl was Justine, who did die for the monster's crime.** I put the tiny necklace in her dress pocket. The girl moved slightly as I stood over her, so I fled the barn.

Since that night, I've stayed near Geneva, hoping to find you. Now you know my story, Frankenstein. Before you say anything, I demand that you do something for me. As you know, I'm alone in the world, and miserable. But I know one being who would stay with me and be my friend. If you created another beast like me, I would finally have a companion. You must create a woman as ugly and hideous as I am.

Whoa! What a story! Now Victor knows he was right—the monster did kill William, and he was responsible for Justine's death too. But as the beast explained, he wasn't always an evil murderer. Victor has been silent for quite a while, listening to the monster's story. What will he say about the monster's demand?

15
Victor's Promise

Victor has just told Walton the monster's story, using the exact words the monster used. Now Victor is going to explain his own thoughts and actions, just as he did before. From now on, the "I" refers to Victor. Once again, he's our narrator, or storyteller.

The creature finished speaking. I sat back and stared silently at my creation. His words left me shocked and confused.

"You must create a female for me," the monster insisted. "You're the only one who has the power to create life. You did it for me; do it again for my companion."

"I refuse," I finally said. "You sit there and tell me how you killed my brother, and now you want me to help you?" My voice rose in anger. "You want me to create another beast like you, so the two of you can ruin the world with your evil ways? Get out of my sight!"

The beast jumped up, squeezing his hands into giant fists. Then he relaxed. "No," the monster said, shaking his head. "I won't threaten you, though I could crush your skull like a berry in the woods. I want you to understand me, not be afraid of me. I'm not evil just to be evil. I'm like this because I'm so miserable. I'm alone. Even you—my creator—would destroy me if you could. You would hurl me from this icy peak and glow with pleasure as my bones smashed against the rocks. Any human would. Am I supposed to enjoy living with your hatred and fear?"

The monster paused. His eyes filled with sadness. "But if I had just one friend," the monster went on, "one living being who accepted me the way I am, I could be happy. Make me that friend, and I'll leave you alone." The creature moved closer. His sadness was replaced by a wicked expression, which crawled up the monster's distorted face. The beast's black lips turned down and his yellow eyes became slits. "If you don't do as I say, you'll be very sorry, I promise you."

He turned away from me. Before I could respond he began to speak again. Now, the monster's voice was calmer. His anger had faded. "I don't want to use such harsh words," the beast said. "I don't want anger to cloud my thoughts. If one human showed me kindness, I would be grateful to all humans. My request is fair. All I want is a companion like me. If I had a mate, I would go to some remote part of the world and never bother humans again. With a mate, I could taste happiness for the first time. I would be thankful, finally, to you, the man who created me and caused my suffering."

I felt the pain in the creature's voice and saw a tear streak the beast's yellow skin. As much as it frightened me to think about another monster in the world, maybe I did owe the monster this deed. After all, he hadn't asked for life. I had given it, then left the creature to face a cruel world. And I could see he had strong emotions and good intentions. It was fair for me to give my creation a little happiness, even if he had committed a terrible crime. And if I didn't agree to help the beast, what kind of terror might he unleash? The beast was strong enough and smart enough to slaughter hundreds of people without ever being caught.

"I'll do it," I said slowly, "on one condition. After I make this female, you'll keep your promise. The two of you must leave Europe and stay away from humans forever."

The monster's black lips curved into a smile. "I swear, once I have my friend, you'll never see me again. I want you to start right away. Go home and begin your work. I'll be watching you, and when you're done, I'll know it."

Before I could say another word, the creature bolted out of the hut and ran down the icy slopes. I found my mule and began to descend the mountain, thinking about the amazing story I'd just heard. Different emotions swirled through my mind. Hatred, fear, and guilt all jumbled together. Then I realized what I had done. I'd promised to create another living being from dead limbs. I thought I had left that horrible, filthy work behind forever. Now it would haunt me again.

Night fell before I reached the village, so I stayed in a tiny hut along the path. The stars didn't cheer me. I looked at them through endless tears, and my shouts of agony filled the night. In the morning, I returned to the inn, gathered my things, and immediately left for Geneva.

My family had already returned to the city. When I arrived home, Elizabeth greeted me at the door. Her warm hug soothed me, but I couldn't forget the job I was supposed to start. "Victor," she gasped. "You look awful. Your eyes are bloodshot and you're so thin! What happened in the mountains?"

I waved her aside. "It wasn't a good trip," I said wearily. "Not what I expected. It's good to be home and feel safe again."

But I could never feel truly safe, knowing my creature was watching my every move.

Can Victor do what the beast wants? Will the monster keep his promise and leave forever if Victor makes him a mate? Victor hopes so, but how can he ever know for sure?

16
Return to the Graveyards

Victor has spent many days telling Captain Walton about the monster. At times, Walton doesn't know if he can believe Victor's amazing tale. But when he sees the fear in Victor's eyes as he talks about the beast, Walton knows it must be true.

"So you set out to build another creature," Walton said.

"I had to," Victor replied. "It was the only thing the beast had ever asked of me. But you can imagine that my heart wasn't really in it."

"Did you do your work in Geneva?" Walton asked.

"No. I decided to go to England. I had heard of scientists there who had done new experiments in biology and anatomy. Their work would make my ghastly chore a little easier. But before I told anyone about my trip, my father called me in for a little talk."

As I entered the library, I had no idea what was on my father's mind. "Victor," he said cautiously, "I know this has been a difficult year for you, and for all of us. But I've been thinking about you and Elizabeth."

"What about her, Papa?" I asked.

"I know you promised your mother you would

marry Elizabeth. I was wondering if you still plan on it. You haven't met someone else, have you?"

"Oh, no, Papa. Of course not. Elizabeth is the perfect woman for me. I love her more than anything in the world."

Mr. Frankenstein smiled. "Good, good! Then I know the perfect thing to bring some happiness back to this family—a wedding. Soon, if possible. I'm not a young man anymore. I don't want to miss that special day. What do you think?"

I hesitated. How could I take the time to get married when I had my new work to do? But I couldn't explain that to my father. I had to make the second creature as soon as possible, so the two beasts would leave me alone forever. Then I could marry Elizabeth in peace.

"Actually, Papa, there's something I'd like to do first. I want to go to England."

Mr. Frankenstein looked surprised. "England? What for?"

"There's some research I want to do there for a new project."

"So, you're finally returning to your work," Mr. Frankenstein said with approval. "That's a good sign. Maybe you'll forget all your sadness once and for all."

"I suppose so," I said, although I didn't really believe it.

"Well," Mr. Frankenstein said jovially, "I don't mind waiting—if Elizabeth doesn't mind."

Elizabeth agreed that I should go to England. Then we would get married. I began making plans for the trip. Elizabeth began making plans too—for our wedding.

"I think we should have the ceremony outside, by the lake," Elizabeth said. "Don't you think so?"

"Whatever you want, dear," I replied. "I just want

to make you happy." Yes, we could have a beautiful wedding by the lake, if my monster was far away, off with his own mate.

"You won't stay in England for too long, will you?" Elizabeth asked. "I can't bear the thought of being parted from you again."

"I will be gone only as long as I need to for my work," I said. "Believe me, Elizabeth, I wouldn't take this trip unless it were absolutely necessary. I'll be home as soon as I can."

To surprise me, Elizabeth and my father made secret arrangements for Henry Clerval to join me on my trip. We were to meet in Strasbourg. **Strasbourg is a city in France, near the German border.** I tried to hide my disappointment with this plan. Normally I loved having Henry as a traveling companion, but on this trip, I needed to be alone. I couldn't let Henry know about my work. I would have to get away from Henry when we reached England.

Finally, I was ready to leave. As I put my bags in the carriage, I thought about Elizabeth and my father alone in the house. They had no idea an enemy might be close by. I imagined the monster breaking into the house and attacking them as they slept. I could see his enormous yellow hands squeezing Elizabeth's slender white neck. Then I remembered what the monster said in the mountains: "I'll be watching you." I shuddered as I heard the words in my head. For now, I was the one who had the most to fear.

I kissed a tearful Elizabeth good-bye and left for France. Henry met me in Strasbourg and we set off for England. Henry was bubbling with excitement about the trip. I, however, was silent and gloomy as I thought about the work I had to do. When Henry saw a tree, he

called out its name and marveled at its beauty. Looking at the same tree, I could only imagine my beast hiding behind it, watching my travels.

A few weeks later, we arrived in London. I rented a room and reluctantly started my research, while Henry spent his days planning a trip to India. I tried to be alone as much as possible. I was too depressed and worried to enjoy being with others, even Henry.

I worked every day for months. During the day, I studied. At night, I slipped out to search for organs and limbs. Every visit to the cemeteries was torture, like stepping into a vat of boiling oil. Just thinking about what I was doing made my heart beat wildly.

The monster was always in my thoughts. I could feel the beast watching me. Once I saw a movement in the shadows of a dark alley. I crept into the narrow lane, ready to confront him. "Stop this!" I cried. "Leave me alone. I'm doing what you want. Can't you leave me alone?"

I jumped back as something rattled the boxes piled in the alley. A small black cat emerged from the garbage, puzzled by my outburst. I couldn't even laugh at my foolishness. The next time, it could be the monster hiding there, waiting to torment me.

I worried for Henry too. When Henry went out alone, sometimes I followed in case the monster attacked my friend. Each day, my fears grew.

One afternoon, I received a letter from a scientist I had met in Geneva. He invited me to visit him in Scotland. Henry was eager to go too, but I insisted I go by myself. Henry's face sagged with disappointment.

"Oh, come on, Henry," I said. "You've found plenty to do here in London. And I think I need some time alone. I want to explore all those Scottish lakes and mountains. Maybe the sights will lift my spirits." And maybe in those desolate regions, I thought, I could find the right place to do my evil work.

I carefully packed all my equipment and the body parts I had found. Henry and I traveled together to Edinburgh. **That's the capital of Scotland.** I met my scientist friend, and then Henry and I separated. I traveled to the far northern corner of the country. I still hadn't seen the monster, but I knew he was close by. The creature had said he would know when his partner was complete. He must have realized that day was getting closer.

I rented a room and a small cottage on a tiny

island off the Scottish coast. Only five people lived
there. The soil was too rocky to grow crops or raise
sheep, and all the food had to come from the mainland,
five miles away. I knew it was the perfect place to
perform my terrible task.

I set up my equipment in the cottage, thinking
about my first laboratory. Back then, my work excited
me. This time, however, I felt sick when I looked at the
body parts in front of me. I avoided looking out the
window because I always expected to see the beast
staring in, watching and waiting for his mate. As I
worked, my lungs ached, as if I were breathing a deadly
fog, and my stomach knotted in pain. The horror of my
work sometimes kept me from entering my lab. I
couldn't bear to face what I was creating. At other times,
I worked fiendishly for days in a row, eager to finish the
project once and for all.

As the creature took shape, I tried to be hopeful.
"This will be good," I told myself. "When this is done,
the beast will be gone forever." But something made me
doubt my own words. I still wondered if the beast
would keep his promise, or if I was creating a second
monster that would destroy the innocent and terrorize
the world. I would have my answer soon enough. In
another day, the she-beast would be complete.

**What can Victor do? He promised his monster a mate, and
now she is almost done. But can he trust the monster? Will
the two creatures go off by themselves? Or will they
slaughter innocent people, as Victor fears? The answer is
just a page away!**

17

Once a Creator, Now a Destroyer

I worked feverishly all that night and the next day. Dusk approached, and the red sun slid below the distant hills. I stepped back from my work and stared out the window. I watched the moon begin to climb above the sea. Slowly, I looked back down at the figure in front of me.

"I can't do it!" I cried aloud. "When I did this horrible work three years ago, I created a monstrous fiend! Because of me and my work, innocent people have died. How can I do this again?"

If I finished this new creature, how could I know what she'd be like? She could turn out to be a hundred times more evil than the first monster. Could I even trust my first creation? Would he and his mate really leave peacefully and never bother humans again? I imagined the horror of two hideous creatures running through the countryside, destroying everything around them.

One last thought made me shudder and my knees go weak. What if the two monsters could somehow have children? The evil would not end for years! "Enough!" I shouted. "I won't create more terror. A hundred years from now, I don't want people to curse the name Frankenstein."

I pulled back my arm, ready to knock the test tubes and equipment off the table. As I turned my head, I saw something move outside the window. My arm froze in midair. The moonlight cast an eerie glow on a shape just beyond the laboratory. The shape moved closer to the glass. It was the thing I had been dreading for so long. I saw the huge, scarred face of the monster. The beast grinned devilishly at me. "I'm glad to see you're hard at work," the monster's voice boomed through the window.

"That's right," I replied. "I'm working to destroy what I've done—just as I should have destroyed you!" With a blur of motion, I wiped the table clean. Glass shattered on the rough stone floor of the laboratory. Outside the window, the monster's grin faded. His lips widened in horror, then pulled tight. His yellowish skin seemed to bubble with anger.

"What are you doing?" the monster screamed.

"Watch, just watch!" I shouted back. I ripped off the arms I had attached to the female's body. I shredded any body parts I saw, then threw the pieces to the floor. For a moment, I felt a great sense of power. I was in control again, not the monster! But as I finished my wild outburst, I heard the monster shriek with anger. He rattled the window with his immense, fleshy fingers, then bolted off into the darkness.

I stood silently for a moment. I took huge gasps of breath, waiting for the creature to burst into the room. But everything was quiet. I studied the mess on the floor, and my head began to spin. I thought I might faint. I staggered out of the lab and ran to my apartment. No one—no thing—waited for me in the night.

When I finally reached my room, I stared out the window and tried to calm down. I watched the moon reflect off the flat sea. The night was quiet. In the distance, a few boats sailed silently on the water. Then I heard a small splash in the water. The sound came again and again, like a drumbeat, coming closer to the shore. Oars, I thought. Someone was rowing toward my apartment.

The paddling stopped. I heard a boat reach the beach, followed by heavy footsteps on the rocks. The steps came closer to the building. I sat in my chair, fear pinning me down. I prayed the steps would pass by. Instead, I heard a creak downstairs. Someone was opening the door.

I couldn't move. I felt like my whole body was tightly wrapped in a rope that cut into my skin. The bedroom door opened slowly. The monster approached, his hands reaching out toward my paralyzed body. "You destroyed her," the monster said, his voice low and rough. "You broke your promise."

"Y-yes, I did," I said, trying to sound strong. "I won't make another evil creature like you. I won't make another murderer."

"I've followed you for months, going hungry and living like an animal," the monster growled. "I waded across rivers and climbed steep hills. My body ached at night, and I often slept in drenching rain. I had just one goal: to be nearby when my friend was complete. I wanted to experience joy at the moment you ended my misery. Now you have made me suffer again." The beast rose to his full height, his head scraping the ceiling. He stepped closer to me. "Don't you realize the power I have over you?" the monster asked, his voice rising. "You created me, Victor Frankenstein, but I am your master now. You must do as I say!"

"Never!" I shouted. I felt a new strength surge through my body. "I'm not afraid of what you can do to me."

"Every creature has a mate," the monster said. "All I

wanted was a partner too, someone like me. How can you deny me that? You have Elizabeth to love, you share her warmth, yet it's all right for me to be alone?"

The monster came closer. "Tonight you destroyed my one chance for happiness. You destroyed the creature that could have been my friend. I will never let you forget what you've done to me. Wherever you go, I'll be there, watching you, waiting for the right time. You will pay, Frankenstein!"

"Stop!" I said. "Stop all these threats and your evil hatred. I did what I had to do."

"And I will do what I have to do," the monster said, his voice now quiet. "Just when you think everything in your life is good, be ready. On a night when you're happy, I will make you and your loved ones miserable. Perhaps...on your wedding night."

I bolted to my feet. "My wedding night?"

"Oh, yes. I will be with you on your wedding night." The monster didn't wait for me to respond. He quickly went through the doorway and ran down the stairs.

I paced around the room, my heart pounding. The monster's awful face danced in front of my eyes. And in my mind, I heard the beast's words: *I will do what I have to do...I will be with you on your wedding night....*

Victor trembled in his chair as he repeated the monster's warning.

"Are you all right?" Walton asked, rising to comfort his friend.

"Yes, yes," Victor said weakly. He fumbled for a glass of water on the table. "But I'm afraid I can't go on tonight. I'm too exhausted. Is that all right?"

"Of course," Walton replied.

18
Victor's Next Journey

The next day, Victor begins his story again. Walton is eager to know what happened to the beast, and to learn what Victor did next on the remote Scottish island.

As the monster ran outside, I went to the window and watched the beast jump into his boat and row into the night. I kept thinking about the creature's words. Would he return on my wedding night to kill me? "That must be it," I said to myself. "The beast wants Elizabeth to suffer and be alone, just as he suffers now."

But I wasn't ready to admit defeat. The beast might be stronger than me, but I was driven by hatred. I had a new mission now. I would hunt down the monster and kill him.

I looked out the window and saw a faint light reflecting off the ocean. The sun was about to rise— once again I'd been up all night. I went outside and walked along the beach, then fell asleep on the sand. When I awoke a few hours later, I saw a fishing boat coming ashore. One of the island residents jumped off and handed me a letter. I ripped open the envelope and began to read:

> *Dear Victor,*
>
> *Hope your work is going well. Are you ready for a break? I'll be in Perth in a week. Meet me there if you can.*
>
> *Best regards,*
> *Henry*

I smiled when I finished reading. I was glad to hear from 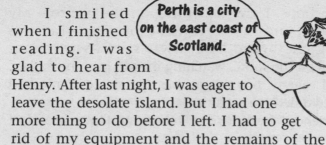 Henry. After last night, I was eager to leave the desolate island. But I had one more thing to do before I left. I had to get rid of my equipment and the remains of the second monster.

Perth is a city on the east coast of Scotland.

I ran over to the small cottage and entered it slowly. I didn't want to see those limbs again. For the first time, body parts revolted me. I smelled death and decay. Holding the organs and limbs as far away from me as I could, I packed the pieces in a basket and loaded rocks on top. Then I hauled the basket to a small boat near the cottage and set sail.

When I could no longer see the tiny island, I pushed the basket off the side of the boat. I felt like a criminal committing a foul crime. But I sighed with relief as the basket gurgled, then sank below the water. "No one will ever find that," I assured myself. "No one will know the horrible thing I tried to do here."

Night had fallen. Clouds passed by the moon and the air was cool, but I felt peaceful on the water. All I heard was the boat sliding across the waves. The sound hypnotized me. In few minutes, I fell asleep.

When I awoke, the sun burned brightly above me. I'd been drifting for hours, and the wind had carried me farther out to sea. The waves tossed the boat and seasickness overwhelmed me. "I'm going to die here," I said to myself. "The monster will have his revenge and not even know it."

But as the waves crashed against the boat and I

gave up hope, I saw something on the horizon. My heart rose, and I cried tears of joy. The wind was pushing me toward land. I was safe! I saw figures standing on the shore, watching me sail into the harbor. I waved eagerly, but the people just stared at me and muttered quietly to each other.

"Friends," I called out. "Where am I? I've been lost at sea."

"You'll find out soon enough," an old man said. He spoke in a hoarse voice, and he squinted at me with a cruel gaze. "There's a magistrate nearby who'll tell you where you are." **A magistrate is a local government official who enforces the law, sort of like a policeman and a judge rolled into one.**

"Magistrate?" I asked, slightly confused. "What's going on?"

"We don't know," the man said, "but maybe you do. Perhaps you can tell us about the dead body we found last night." **Another murder! We know Victor didn't do it—he was drifting at sea. Who's the victim? And who's the killer?**

When I came ashore, the people led me to the center of the town and the magistrate's office. The man looked like a kind grandfather, with his silver hair and round cheeks, but he glared at me suspiciously. "My name's Kirwin," he said gruffly. "Who are you, and where have you come from?"

"I am Victor Frankenstein. I sailed last night from Scotland." I tried to sound confident. "Where am I?"

"You're in Ireland," Kirwin replied. "From what I

hear, you might know something about a murder. Last night, one of our fishermen found a body near the beach. He thought maybe someone had drowned, then washed ashore. But the body was dry. The man was killed on land. Do you know anything about it?"

"I told you, I was at sea last night," I insisted. "How could I know anything?"

"You're a stranger," Kirwin said. "We don't get many strangers stopping by here. First we find a dead man, then you appear. Should I believe this is a coincidence?"

I tried to repeat my innocence, but the magistrate cut me off. "Don't say anything more," Kirwin said. "I want you to do something for me. Take a look at the body and see if you recognize the man."

I followed Kirwin through the streets to the doctor's house. A crowd gathered around us. The townspeople pointed at me and scowled.

"You say the man didn't drown," I said as I walked behind Kirwin. "How did he die?"

"Strangled," the magistrate replied. "He had the life squeezed right out of him. We saw terrible black marks all over his throat."

"Black marks?" I thought of William—his throat had black marks on it too! The monster had to be nearby. I clenched my fists in disgust and rage. But the beast had threatened to kill my loved ones. Why would he kill a stranger, someone who meant nothing to me?

We entered the doctor's house. "In here," the magistrate said, leading me to a coffin. I trembled as I approached and looked inside.

"Oh my God!" I cried. "No, no, it can't be!" I

collapsed on the coffin, falling onto the lifeless body of Henry Clerval.

No! Not Henry! He's Victor's lifelong friend! The monster has killed another of Victor's loved ones, just as he said he would. And if that's not bad enough, Kirwin and the townspeople think Victor committed the murder. What is Victor going to do?

19
A Growing Fear

The people in this seaside town are sure Victor is the murderer, so they put him in jail. All Victor can do is wait for his trial—and think about his murdered friend and the monster.

Alone in my dark, damp cell, I cried day and night for Henry. After seeing my friend's cold body stretched out in the coffin, I slipped into madness again, and a fever made my whole body burn. I rarely slept, and when I did, I dreamed of the people who had died because of my beast.

"William!" I cried out in my nightmares. "I killed you...and Justine...and now Henry too. All of you are dead because of me!" I awoke from those horrible dreams drenched in sweat, and I hated myself for what I had done.

"I should be dead, not them," I said to myself. "Why should I survive, after all I've done to the people I love?"

I spent two months alone and tormented by my guilt. My trial approached. Kirwin, the magistrate, must have felt sorry for me. He could see how sick I was, and he moved me to a more comfortable cell.

One day, Kirwin entered my cell smiling. "I have good news for you," he said. "You have a visitor."

I hunched down in a corner of the cell. Who knew I was here? It could only be the monster. Had the monster somehow convinced Kirwin to let him visit me? "No, I won't see him!" I shouted. "Send him away!" Still exhausted from my illness, I couldn't bear the idea of confronting my creation again.

Kirwin was puzzled. "I don't know who you think is here, but I would have thought you'd be happy to see a friendly face after all these months. I wrote to your father and told him you were here. He's come to see you."

"Papa!" I sighed. "Yes, yes, send him in!"

"Victor!" Mr. Frankenstein said, rushing into the cell. "Victor, how did you end up like this? And poor Henry! It's so terrible—"

I burst into tears when I heard my dead friend's name. "Oh, Papa, I can't talk about him now."

"You're sick again, Victor. I can tell. We'll get you out of here. There are witnesses from Scotland who are going to testify for you. They'll tell the judge you were in Scotland, just like you said, so you couldn't have killed Henry. You'll be free, and then we can go back to Geneva for your wedding. Everything will be all right, you'll see."

Mr. Frankenstein was right. The witnesses supported Victor's story. He was found innocent and released. A relieved Victor and his father returned to Geneva.

I was glad to be going home so I could finally see Elizabeth again. But as my father chatted happily about the future, my mind was filled with the horrors of the past. I saw Henry's gray face, with those deep black marks on his throat. And I remembered the promise I had made to the monster—a promise I had broken. When I did think about the future, I could only see the creature waiting to kill again.

My father and I spent some time in Paris. While we were there, I received a letter from Elizabeth.

Dearest Victor,

I'm happy to know you are finally on your way home. Henry's death was a terrible shock to all of us. I can only imagine how it destroyed you. But I want to forget about the awful past and write about the future, our future. I hope the thought of it excites you as much as it does me.

I know we both want to be married, but sometimes I fear you may have met someone else. Tell me this isn't true. I want to know that we will marry because you love me, not because you are honoring your mother's dying wish. When you return home, I will know the answer when I see your face. Your smile will tell me everything.

Elizabeth

Elizabeth's letter made me smile, but only for a moment. Then I remembered the beast and his warning: *I will be with you on your wedding night.* I was certain the monster had chosen that night to kill me. I prayed I could kill the creature first.

I wrote back to Elizabeth and assured her she was the only woman I loved. I also wrote the following words:

I have something I must tell you, Elizabeth. It is a dreadful secret, and when you hear it, you'll understand why my life has been so miserable this past year. The horror I must confess will chill your bones, but I can't reveal my story yet. The day after we are married, I will tell you everything. I want you to know the truth. But until then, you must never mention this secret or try to make me talk about it.

A week later, my father and I finally arrived home. Elizabeth was waiting for us. "Victor," she called out warmly, running to hug me.

"My love," I said. During my time in jail, I hadn't thought of Elizabeth very often. Now I realized how much I had missed her.

"You're so thin," Elizabeth said, fighting back tears. "And you're still sick."

I nodded. "My body and my heart both ache. I could sleep for months."

"We've been through so much this past year," Elizabeth said sadly. "Now we deserve to be happy. We should think of nothing but our wedding night and how wonderful it will be."

I tried to smile and not think about those two terrible words: *wedding night.*

The wedding day approached quickly. On the outside, I was calm. I laughed when friends dropped by to offer congratulations. I helped Elizabeth with the plans for the honeymoon. But in my heart, I dreaded the wedding. My fear grew each day. I walked around the house, peering into dark corners. When a curtain rustled, I ran to the window to make sure the monster wasn't there. I scanned the yard constantly, looking for any sign of the creature. Once, out of the corner of my eye, I saw something move. I jumped and clutched my chest. It was only the shadow of a tree moving in the wind. I finally started carrying a gun to defend myself against the monster, but I never saw the beast, and nothing happened. As the days passed, I actually relaxed a bit and began to look forward to the wedding.

I rose early on the morning of the wedding. As I dressed, I could feel the sun's warmth through my open window.

"What a gorgeous day," Elizabeth said as she took my hand. We walked to the lake, where our friends and family waited for the ceremony to begin.

"Maybe nature is blessing our wedding," I said.

Our family and friends celebrated all day. I hadn't been surrounded by so much happiness and love in years. Late in the afternoon, Elizabeth and I said good-bye to everyone and climbed into a small boat. We sailed across the lake to an inn on the far shore.

As we sailed, I watched the sun nestle between two mountain peaks. Then the orange ball disappeared from view. The stiff wind faded into a soft breeze.

"Are you happy, dear?" Elizabeth asked.

"Of course," I said. "It's been a perfect day."

"And we still have the night ahead of us," Elizabeth reminded me.

"Yes, our wedding night." I said softly. The words brought my agony out of its hiding place in my heart. All the love and joy I'd felt that day drained out of me, and terror took its place. My skin crawled. An icy touch of fear washed over my body and my hands trembled.

"Are you cold, Victor?" Elizabeth asked.

"Y-yes," I said, my teeth chattering. "Just a little."

"Well, we'll be there soon," she said, smiling.

Too soon, I thought. As fear shook my body, I wondered if those feelings would torment me for as long as I lived. And as I studied my wife's calm, beautiful face, I wondered exactly how long I had left to live.

What will Victor find when he reaches the shore? Is the monster waiting there, ready to keep his terrible promise?

20
"...On Your Wedding Night"

With each minute, the sky grew darker and my fears grew. The moon struggled to cast light, but thick, angry clouds rolled in. The clouds reminded me of a flock of hungry vultures blotting out the sun as they followed the smell of death. The wind gained speed, whipping up waves on the lake. A howling noise filled my ears. I looked all around us. Was that my monster's cry taunting me, telling me he was near? The horrible sound rang out again. No, it was just a powerful gust from the strengthening storm. Suddenly, the black clouds split open and a heavy rain pounded the lake.

Uh-oh—we know that's not a good sign.

We reached the shore and ran for the safety of the inn. As I ran, I looked all around, searching for the beast's presence. I patted my jacket, feeling for the pistol hidden underneath it.

"Is something wrong, Victor?" Elizabeth asked with concern.

"No, no, everything's fine." I tried to sound calm,

but my voice had a nervous edge. "After tonight, everything will be fine."

"You've been acting strangely since we left Geneva," Elizabeth said. "Does this have anything to do with...your secret?"

My eyes widened with horror. "Please, Elizabeth, I beg you. Don't ask me about that. Tomorrow, I'll tell you everything. But tonight..."

"Yes?"

I looked away. "Tonight is our wedding night. We must be happy while we can."

Elizabeth looked at me oddly, as if I had uttered some wild ramblings in a foreign language. But she said nothing and headed for our room. I remained in the lobby, pacing all around. The clerk seemed suspicious, so I slowly set off for our room. I crept down the halls, staying close to the wall. I constantly spun around to see if the beast was sneaking up from behind me. Whenever I saw a half-opened door, I slowly pushed it open and searched the darkness for signs of life. I listened for the monster's heavy breathing or the shuffle of his feet. All I heard was my own blood pounding in my ears.

As I walked up the stairs, a piercing scream shattered the quiet. I leaped the steps two at a time. I heard another scream, louder and more frightening.

I burst into the room, my gun in my hand. Elizabeth's limp body hung over the side of the bed. Her hair half-covered her face, which was frozen in horror, like a statue.

"Elizabeth!" I gasped. I stepped toward her, then fainted and crumpled to the floor.

When I woke up, I was surrounded by the other guests at the inn. They stood quietly, horrified by Elizabeth's dead body. Someone had moved her so she now lay flat on her back. I shook my head, not believing what I saw.

"She's just asleep," I mumbled, getting up to hold her. "Just asleep."

But as soon as I touched her hand, I knew my darling Elizabeth was dead. Her skin felt like an icy slab of marble. I looked at her face, at the perfect curve of her cheek. Then I saw the purplish-black marks on her throat, and I knew the monster's deadly hands had touched her skin. It was Elizabeth the monster wanted to kill all along, not me. I had destroyed the monster's partner, so he destroyed mine.

I turned my tear-stained cheek and rested it on Elizabeth's chest. From here I could see the window. The sky had cleared, and moonlight streamed through the open curtain. Suddenly, through the window, I saw the gigantic form of my monster!

The creature laughed when he saw me lying beside my dead bride. The beast pointed at the dead body, taunting me. The fiend's devilish laughter flamed my anger. I jumped up and fired my gun, but the monster was too quick for me. He had already jumped off the window ledge and headed toward the lake.

"There's someone outside!" I yelled. "The murderer! After him!"

Some of the guests and I rushed outside. We combed the woods by the water's edge, but we didn't see the monster. I sensed he was nearby, enjoying my hopeless search. As I walked through the woods, my eyesight turned hazy, as if a gray fog had settled on top of me. My head began to spin and I collapsed under a tree. The guests carried me back to the inn. My body burned with a fever, and tears filled my eyes. I sat alone in my room, crying all through the night. "Elizabeth," I groaned. "I've killed you too. I will have my revenge for you, and for the others. The monster must die!"

"Good Lord!" Walton exclaimed. "Your beautiful Elizabeth—"

"Yes, my beautiful Elizabeth," Victor said, fighting back tears. "The one pure thing in my life, and the beast destroyed her. But even then, he wasn't done ruining me. Let me continue."

"Certainly," Walton said. He sat on the edge of his chair, amazed by each new twist in Victor's incredible story.

I returned to Geneva the next day, seething with hatred. I would have ripped the beast apart with my bare hands if the creature stood in front of me. At home, I entered my father's room slowly, dreading what I had to tell him.

"Victor," he said with surprise. "What are you doing here? Where is Elizabeth? What about your honeymoon?"

"Papa, it's too terrible," I wailed.

My father grabbed my shoulders. "What? Is it Elizabeth?"

"Yes," I stammered through my tears. "She—she's dead. Murdered!

My father cried as if he had been shot. "No, it can't be! Not my beautiful daughter!" His eyes filled with tears as they stared into mine. "Why?" he cried. "Why have all these tragedies struck our family? For what crime are we being punished with all these deaths?"

I couldn't tell him it was because of my crime that the Frankensteins suffered so. Papa grabbed his head and screamed in agony. Then he collapsed at my feet. I rushed him to bed and called a doctor, but it was too late. The news had shattered my father and now he was dead too. I beat my fists on the walls, tears blurring my vision. From deep inside me, my pain shot up through my body, and I wailed with grief.

"You devil!" I shouted, cursing my creation. "You might as well have crushed the old man with your hands." But as I said those words, I knew my hands had made the beast, so I was responsible too. I had only one reason left to live: to track down the beast and kill it.

But my mission had to wait. The deaths of my beloved Elizabeth and my father were too much to bear. I slipped into a feverish madness once again. I spent months in a hospital, locked in a room no bigger than a cell. I dreamed of summer days from my childhood, but the dreams always turned into black nightmares filled with death.

When I was finally healthy again, I prepared to leave Geneva forever and hunt down my monster. Before I left, I visited the cemetery where my family was buried. The night was dark and deathly quiet. I shivered as I walked through the graveyard. I saw William's tombstone and the two fresh graves for Elizabeth and my father. I flung myself on the ground. "Elizabeth, Papa," I shouted through my tears. "If you can hear me, I promise I will get my revenge. The demon will die—or I will die trying to find him." I pounded the earth with my hands.

I lay there for a few minutes. I didn't hear anything except my own quiet sobs. Then, a sound cut through the night. "Laughter?" I wondered. "Was that laughter? Who could be laughing here?" But I didn't have to ask—I knew.

The monster's fiendish howl echoed across the

graveyard. The sound made my body shake. Only the laughter of my diabolical creature could make me shiver like that. **Diabolical means something completely and totally evil, like the monster is now.**

"Good, good," the monster finally called out to me. "I'm glad you still have a reason to live. The longer you live, the more I can make you suffer."

"Beast!" I cried. I jumped up and ran after the creature, but he slipped away into darkness.

From that instant, I began my chase. I followed the creature across Europe, always just behind him. The monster wasn't afraid of being caught. To him, the chase was like a child's game. He scribbled little messages on trees so I would know which way to go.

"Follow me!" one note said. "I'm running north, to frozen lands. The cold won't bother me. But can you survive?"

I headed north. If the beast went to the coldest corners of the earth or the steamiest tropics, I had to follow. My desire for revenge helped me survive any obstacle I found. Once, years before, I was totally devoted to creating a living being. Now, I was equally devoted to destroying that same creature.

I stayed with friendly villagers I met along the way. Some shook with fear as they told me about the horrible creature they had seen run through the woods just days before. Those stories told me I was on the right track.

Finally, the monster led me to the Arctic Ocean. I bought a sled and some dogs and headed across the ice. As bitter air clawed at my skin, I could see the monster on his own sled. For weeks I traveled behind him, never able to catch up. The Arctic winds stung my face and my hands ached from the cold. I ate very little, and my tired bones struggled to stand. In my darkest moments,

I cried out in despair. I feared I would never catch him. But my hatred kept me going. My suffering meant nothing when I thought about the horrible deaths of my loved ones.

I traveled for weeks across the ice. Sometimes I heard the sea rumble beneath me, and the ice shifted below my sled. One day, the rumble turned into a roar. Water shot up around me as the ice broke into jagged pieces. I clung to one of them, fighting for my life.

"The hunt is over," I cried. "The beast has won again."

I prepared to die. Suddenly, in the distance, I thought I saw a black speck moving across the white background that surrounded me. "If I can just hold on," I murmured through frozen lips. "Just hold on..."

Meanwhile, the monster and his sled raced across the frozen land.

I bet I know what that black speck was. A ship! Captain Walton's ship. Victor was about to be rescued. You read about that event back at the beginning of the story, remember?

21
Death on the Ice

Victor is done telling Walton his story about the monster and how they ended up in the Arctic. What does the captain think of all this? Does he believe Victor? Let's see.

Walton sat back and shook his head. He felt like he'd just swum ten miles in the icy Arctic waters. His body ached and shivered, and his head pounded. Could this tale be true? "It's an incredible story," the captain finally said.

"It's a true story," said Victor. "Now I want to ask you a favor. Will you do it?"

Walton studied Victor's dark, determined eyes. "That depends," he replied.

"If I die," Victor said, "I want you to continue my chase. You must find the monster and kill him for me."

"Well, I—"

Victor's words spilled out of him in a rush. "I want you to take your sword and thrust it through his heart. As you do so, call out the names of everyone he has killed: William, Justine, Henry, Elizabeth, my father, and finally, me—Victor Frankenstein. My spirit will be near you to guide your hand."

Walton fidgeted in his seat. The whole story was

too horrible. Then he remembered the huge figure he had seen speeding across the ice. It didn't look human. And even though Victor acted like a madman at times, shouting with rage at the monster, Walton felt his friend was a good, honest man.

"How did you do it?" Walton asked, ignoring Victor's request for help. "How did you bring dead flesh to life?"

Victor jumped out of his chair. "Don't even think about such things! Do you want to know so you can try to create your own murderous demon? I would never tell anyone how it is done. Look at how that knowledge has ruined me!"

Walton sat back, surprised at the outburst. "I only wanted to know because—"

"No," Victor said sternly. "That hideous knowledge will die with me." He fell back into his chair, his energy drained. "Once," he said softly, "I thought that I would do something great with my life. But instead of being a great scientist, I'm a wretched thing myself."

Breathing heavily, Victor drew closer to Walton. "Do you know why I stay alive?" he asked. "There's only one reason—to destroy the monster I created." Victor slumped in his chair, exhausted. Walton led him to his bed. The captain knew what his friend would dream about that night. **I know what Victor will dream about too—the monster. Walton hates to see Victor so upset, but the captain has his own problems. His ship is stuck in the ice again.**

Days passed with the ship stranded in the ice. Walton told Victor his fears.

"Look around us," Walton said. "We're surrounded by mountains of ice. A giant iceberg could crush us to dust at any moment. The men expect me do something, but there's nothing I can do. They trusted me once, but I think some of them have given up. I hear them cry in agony, saying their lives are over. Some have already died, killed by this terrible cold. If we break free, those sailors who are left want to sail for home. I'm afraid there'll be a mutiny if I don't do what they want."

A mutiny is a revolt, or a rebellion. If the sailors don't like what the captain is doing, they lock him up and take over the ship. A mutiny is not Walton's idea of a good time.

"The ice is nothing," Victor said, waving his hand. "Other ships have survived worse, I'm sure. You must stick with your dream, Captain. You can reach the North Pole. I know it."

Some of the men heard Victor's comments. They talked angrily among themselves, then stormed over to Walton. "Captain," one of the men said defiantly, "you can't listen to him."

"What do you mean?" Walton asked.

"If this ice ever breaks," the sailor said, "you'd better turn around and head south. We have to escape while we can. If we keep heading north, it will be suicide."

Victor interrupted before Walton could respond. "What are you saying? Didn't you agree to go with your captain on a glorious adventure?" Victor dripped with sweat. A fever inflamed his body. Walton knew his friend was dying.

"I wish I had your faith and courage," the captain told Victor. "But sometimes we can go too far, as explorers, or as scientists. I can't risk the men's lives. You have seen that a man can go too far in search of knowledge."

Victor shook his head. "If you turn back, I won't go with you. I will continue to hunt my monster." He tried to stand tall, but he fell backward, weak with sickness. The sailors rushed him to his cabin.

Victor's illness got worse during the night. Walton sat with his friend. Suddenly the captain heard a crackling sound and the men cheering on deck.

"The ice has broken!" a sailor cried.

Walton looked at Victor, stretched out like he was already in his coffin. The captain knew he couldn't continue his journey to the North Pole. He went up on deck and told the crew he would turn the ship around in the morning and head for home.

Walton returned to Victor's cabin. He put his head near Victor's chest and listened to his shallow breath. Victor stirred and tried to speak. "I—I will die soon, Walton," he said feebly. "My enemy still lives."

"Don't speak," Walton said softly, touching Victor's shoulder.

"Walton, look at me." Victor struggled with the words. "I failed in my last task. I didn't kill my monster. I ask you to do what I could not. But I understand if you have to return to England. Just remember this one thing: Don't let your desires, your ambitions, ruin you as mine ruined me. Find your happiness in simple things. You may think your search for adventure or knowledge is innocent, like I once did. But look where it can lead."

Victor closed his eyes and didn't speak again. A faint smile came to his lips, then vanished. Walton knew Victor was dead.

Walton returned to his cabin, crying for his dead friend. He'd barely reached his bed when he heard a noise from Victor's cabin. Walton rushed back. Inside, a huge figure stood over Victor's bed.

"Good God!" Walton shouted, stepping back in fright. He had never seen such a horrible sight in his life. The creature's head scraped the cabin's wooden beams. Long black hair clotted with ice hung in ragged strips over the being's face. He stretched one hand toward Victor's body. Walton saw wrinkled skin that looked like the decaying wrappings of an ancient mummy. The monster turned when he heard Walton enter and stared at him.

Victor's story hadn't totally prepared the captain for the ugly creature he saw in front of him. The hideous scars and yellow eyes sickened Walton. The beast looked like it had come from another world. Walton put his hand to his face, afraid to look the monstrous thing in the eyes. The beast headed for the window.

"Don't go!" Walton called, though he didn't know why. Walton knew he could never kill the beast, as Victor had wanted. Walton tried to speak again, but fear made him swallow his words. For some strange reason, Walton was concerned for the beast. He felt like he knew the creature, after hearing Victor's story.

"I wanted him to forgive me," the monster cried. "I came to beg for that forgiveness now, but I am too late.

Frankenstein is dead. I have killed him too. No matter how angry I was, every time I killed I felt pain. Do you think I enjoyed hearing Henry Clerval's dying screams? Do you think the cries of my other victims gave me pleasure? This death hurts worst of all."

Walton finally found the courage to speak. "Should I feel sorry for you?" he asked. "You destroy people one minute, then cry for the suffering you cause the next. You're only sorry Frankenstein died before you could take his life with your own hands."

"No, no, that's not true," the monster said sadly. "I never enjoyed killing. I didn't want to be evil. Look at me—I know I disgust you. But there was a good, decent being inside this body when Frankenstein made me. You heard him talk about my crimes and you think I am wicked. Maybe I was, in those seconds when I was filled with anger and revenge. But I wasn't always like that. When I first entered this world, I enjoyed pleasure and beautiful things. All I wanted was to meet others who could see the goodness inside me."

The monster trembled and pointed at Victor' body. "*He* made me a devilish beast. First he ran from me. And he made me so ugly that no other humans would come close to me. Then he promised to make me a friend, but he destroyed her out of fear. You hate me now too, don't you?"

Walton fumbled for words.

"Don't deny it. I am responsible for your friend's death, and you hate me. But I hate myself more than you could ever hate me. No crime committed on earth will ever match what I have done. I know that, and I am sorry for the pain I caused. All this pain I caused others and myself—it's all because I was unloved and alone."

"What are you going to do now?" Walton asked the beast.

"There's only one thing I can do. I shall die. Frankenstein is dead, so I have no reason to live. I will never kill again. Nor will I ever see the stars shine like diamonds on a fall night, or feel a warm summer breeze tickle my leathery skin. When I entered the world, each sight and sound made me cry with joy. I will never feel that happiness again."

The monster looked over at Victor's body. "He wanted to kill me so others wouldn't suffer. Now I'll do his work for him. I'll leave your ship and sail north.

Then I'll build a funeral pyre. The flames will turn my disgusting body into ash, and the winds will scatter the ashes over the earth." **A funeral pyre is a special fire used to burn dead bodies. In this case, the monster is going to jump into the fire before he's dead.**

Before Walton could respond, the monster jumped through the cabin window. Amazed at what he had seen and heard, Walton watched the monster vanish into the night.

Grady, Walton's assistant, ran into the room. "Captain, the men say they saw someone jump from the ship. They thought he came from here." Grady stopped, noticing Victor's lifeless body. "Sir," he whispered, "is he—?"

Walton nodded. "Yes. My friend is dead." The captain looked out the window and saw the sun's first rays shining off the ice. "And our adventure is over. Grady, prepare the men to set sail. I'll keep my word. We're going home."

Wow! What a tale! And it all started way back, one stormy night when young Mary Shelley had a "waking nightmare." From her imagination came one of the scariest monster stories of all time! Of course, I was never scared. Really, I wasn't. The truth is, I LIKE it here under the sofa . . . .